DEFENDING YVETTE

GHOST, BOOK FOUR

PJ FIALA

DEDICATION

I've had so many wonderful people come into my life and I want you all to know how much I appreciate it. From each and every reader who takes the time out of their day to read my stories and leave reviews, thank you.
My beautiful, smart and fun Road Queens, who play games with me, post fun memes, keep the conversation rolling and help me create these captivating characters, places, businesses and more. Thank you ladies for your ideas, support and love.
The following characters and places were created by:

Patricia Case - Lucian
Tami Czenkus - Wyatt Lawson description
Tami Czenkus and Amy Ball - Ira Stevens
Lois Gehring & Kerry Harteker - Wyatt's sisters Tyler & Gabrielle (Gabby)
Kerry Harteker - Danielle (Dany) Lawson
Karen Hoffman - Runaway - Lola
Barb Keller & Debbie Douglas-Moncrief - Yvette Jacobson
Kim Kurtz - John Caulfield

Nicky Ortiz - Wyatt Lawson
Elena Pietrantonio - Bennet Martin
Janeen Wagner Phillips & Kimberly Slorf Veihl - Emersyn,
Hayden and Elise Copeland

Kerry Harteker assisted with medical terminology and
advice.

A special thank you to Julie Collier, my PA and Deranged
Doctor Designs for this amazing cover.

Last but not least, my family for the love and sacrifices
they have made and continue to make to help me achieve
this dream, especially my husband and best friend, Gene.
Words can never express how much you mean to me, I
Love You.

To our veterans and current serving members of our
armed forces, police and fire departments, thank you
ladies and gentlemen for your hard work and sacrifices;
it's with gratitude and thankfulness that I mention you in
this dedication.

GLOSSARY - GHOST

There are men and women out there who are highly trained and brave, who will go into situations most of us won't. These are the men and women of GHOST - Government Hidden Ops Specialty Team.

Auggie Vickers - Co-Founder of GHOST, Auggie has made his career in the military. He's risen in the ranks many only dream of. He's also a fierce and loyal husband and father. *(To unlock Keirnan (Defending Keirnan also in audiobook)*

Dane Copeland - Co-Founder of GHOST. Single father, retired Army Special Forces. (Defending Keirnan also in audiobook)

Ford Montgomery - 6'2" tall. Army veteran turned bounty hunter. Co-Founder of Big 3 Security. (Finding His Fire also in audiobook)

Lincoln Winters - 6'5" Former Army Ranger. Worked as a detective before co-founding Big 3 Security with Ford and Dodge. (Finding His Mark also in audiobook)

Dodge Sager - 6'2" - Former Army turned State

Trooper before co-founding Big 3 Security. (Finding His Jewel also in audiobook)

Jacqueline (Jax) Masters - 5'6" Army trained before following in her father and brother's footsteps and joining GHOST. (Finding His Jewel also in audiobook)

Gaige Vickers - Son of Auggie Vickers, Gaige is 6'2" of former military and tough as nails. (Defending Sophie also in audiobook)

Hawk Delany - 6'8" dark and broody. Former military and no nonsense. (Defending Roxanne also in audiobook)

Wyatt Lawson - 6'7", dark hair, Medic trained in the military. (Defending Yvette also in audiobook)

Axel Dunbar - 6'2", long dark hair, specializes in recon and undercover work. (Defending Bridget also in audiobook)

Josh Masters - 6' Jax's twin. Army trained, specializes in recon. (Defending Isabella also in audiobook)

DESCRIPTION

GHOST: Government Hidden Ops Specialty Team. They eliminate the threat when no one else can.

When GHOST special operative, Wyatt Lawson, is tasked with helping out the friend of a friend, he decides it's his good deed for the day. It's not his normal offering as he's usually tracking down criminals and putting a stop to crimes. That's what this brawny, gruff man enjoys.

When the friend of a friend, Yvette Jacobson arrives, he finds a beaten and broken woman afraid of her own shadow. Immediately the medic in him jumps into action and begins assessing the damage. As he spends time with Yvette, his protective instincts take over and he finds the damaged beauty alluring.

But when she shares the reason she was beaten and that danger is now likely at his door, Wyatt has no choice but to treat her as any other victim he's worked with and put up defenses to protect his daughter. Despite the fact he's attracted to her, he needs to keep this professional.

When Yvette puts herself in harms way under the pretense that she's saving others, this warrior will move mountains to bring the lovely woman home and make her his. That is if he can get to her in time.

***

Entire series complete!

USA Today bestselling author PJ Fiala brings you the full and complete GHOST series—heroes willing to sacrifice everything in service to their country, and for the women they love. Full length novel with no cliffhanger, no cheating, and a happily-ever-after guaranteed.

Let's stay in touch where bots, algorithms and subjective admins don't decide what we see. PJ Fiala's Readers' Club is my newsletter where I promise to only send you content you enjoy! https://www.subscribepage.com/pjfialafm

1

...high school friend.

...speaker icon on her phone ...tossed it on the bed. She continued hurriedly to throw her clothing into a suitcase as the phone rang on the other end.

"Jax Mas...Sager."

A small giggle sounded after Jax said her name.

"Still not used to your new name?"

"[illegible]"

Pausing from her packing, she swallowed. "I'm in trouble, Jax and I don't know what to do."

"Is that asshole hitting you now?"

Blinking rapidly to stave off the tears she said, "That's not the whole of it and I have to get out of town."

"Okay, come here to Indiana and tell me what's going on. You can stay with Dodge and me."

Relief flooded through her as she sat on the edge of the bed and picked up her phone. "Jax, normally I'd say I don't want to be an imposition, but he's going to kill me. As in literally. I found out what he's into and I'm not safe."

"Have you called the police?"

"They won't keep me safe. One of his good buddies, Ira, works for the local PD and is just as dirty as he is."

"I hate dirty cops. Do you have the means to get here?"

"Yes."

"Okay, text me your arrival time and flight number. I'm on a mission, but I'm only one state away. We're leaving in about an hour, so I should be home before you can get there from Florida."

"Thanks, Jax. Really."

"See ya. Stay safe. Call me if things go south, and I'll see what I can do."

The line went dead-typical Jax. She was never overly sentimental. She also didn't understand what it felt like to fear you couldn't protect yourself. She'd always been so self-assured and able to kick anyone's ass. That's what she was going to have Jax teach her; how to protect herself before it was too late.

She heard a car door slam and peeked out the window making sure to stay hidden. This was the first time she was happy she lived on the third floor. Not seeing anyone, she continued to fill her suitcase with the things she felt she'd need.

She made a quick trip to the bathroom for her toothbrush, body wash and a few necessities; she dropped them in a toiletry bag and tossed that into the suitcase as she walked past for one more trip to her closet.

Her stomach was beginning to turn sour the longer she was in her apartment. A couple pair of jogging pants, leggings, a few tanks, some other tops, skirts, shoes, underwear, and other clothing and she was ready to close it up and get the hell out of here. No time to change out of her business skirt and heels; she'd have to do that later.

A text sounded on her phone and a quick glance told her that her flight was on time. She'd booked it before she called Jax; it was the safest place she could think of going. Zipping her suitcase closed, she slid it off the side of the bed, and pulled up the long handle. Wheeling it down the short hallway to the main living area, she glanced at the clock on the stove. It had been an hour since John had threatened her with bodily harm. Actually, mortal force. Normally he'd just say, "Keep your fucking mouth shut or I'll shut it for you." This time he'd said, "The second I find you I'll kill you, you little snitch." She knew he wasn't lying; she'd gotten in deep this time. Luckily for her, he was out of town, but she was not sure how far away he was or how much time she had; she needed to go now.

A quick glance out of the living room window to her car showed no one walking around, nothing out of place. She unsuccessfully tried to swallow but had no time to wet her throat. Grabbing her purse from the table by the door, she slung it over her shoulder, snatched her suitcase, and stepped out of her apartment. She'd figure out what to do with the apartment once this nightmare was over. Someone could help her get her things, but she doubted she ever could feel safe living here again. Sliding the key in the deadbolt, she twisted the lock and started her trek to the elevator. Debating using it or lugging her suitcase down three flights of stairs, she decided on the elevator. Her feet felt as heavy as lead. She didn't think she was making time since each passing second seemed like an hour.

Finally reaching the elevator, she steered her suitcase into the metal box, jabbed at the down button, and prayed it would close before someone else got on. Attempting to swallow again without luck, she took a deep breath and tried to quell the nausea that felt like acid in her stomach. She jammed her finger on the close door button over and over to hurry her escape from the building.

The ride down was fairly quick. The elevator door opened, a car door slammed, and she jumped. She forced down the rising bile and inhaled deep breaths letting them out slowly. Looking around as she left the building, she tried in vain to stay calm. Nothing could trip her up now mostly because she didn't have the time.

The heat was oppressive and sweat immediately began to trickle down her back. Her hands grew wet, the handle on her suitcase became slippery, but she held on. Right now, these were the only possessions she had in the world for the next few days and she'd be damned if she lost them.

In about three seconds she would burst into tears. Telling herself to hold it together, she repeated a mantra in her head. "I can do this. Be like Jax. I can do this. Be like Jax."

A noise sounded behind her and she turned to see absolutely nothing. She muttered, "I must be losing my mind. Better than my life, I guess."

Glancing in both directions for anything and anyone unusual, she made a beeline for her car. She progressed quickly with the grip on her suitcase now iron clad. The sidewalk seemed strangely uneven as she picked up her pace to get to her car, a sweet little Mercedes that she'd just bought a few months ago. Spotting it only two cars away, she stifled a sob. She was running as fast as she could in her heels; she pushed herself harder because she was almost there. The sweat now dribbled down her face and her vision blurred.

Something jumped on the back of her right leg and

she fell forward, tumbling over her suitcase and sprawling half on the sidewalk and half on the parking lot. The pavement was scorching hot and she felt her skin burning. Then her stomach twisted when she heard the male voice behind her.

"There you are you little bitch."

2

Wyatt pushed up the weights above him. His arms shook, sweat dripped from his temples into his hair, and his drenched back stuck to the bench beneath him. But his eyes continued to look at the words written above him – *You've got this.* It was on a poster fastened on the ceiling above him for inspiration.

Raising the weights completely above him, he counted to five, making sure to not let it shake. He roughly dropped the weights on the rest bar, huffed out a few breaths, then sat up, and hollered, "Yes!"

Axel chuckled, "Congrats, bud you finally benched 300. Took you long enough."

"I'm pumped. Finally achieved that goal. Whew." He stood and swung his arms around to relieve the tightness.

Josh, Jax's twin brother, hopped off the treadmill and fist bumped him. "Nice, Wyatt. Now that you've hit that goal, maybe you'll get your distance running up and be able to beat me."

Laughing, Josh grabbed a towel from the rack and swiped it down his face.

"I'm headed to the showers, gotta date tonight."

Wyatt shook his head as he tossed out a jab, "You getting married next, bro?"

"Fuck, no. Just hoping to get laid."

"Not if your date can see your sorry ass."

Josh chuckled, held up his middle finger, and left the weight room. Axel laughed along with him, grabbed two free weights from the rack, and began doing curls.

"Wyatt, you've still not been able to beat me in the quarter mile. Just sayin'."

"Saving my knee, bro. As I get older, it pains me a bit more. None of us is getting any younger. I know how to exercise it for missions. It's starting to hurt once in a while, and I don't like it."

The compound phone rang. Wyatt stood and grabbed the phone from the wall as he held up his middle finger to Axel.

"Lawson."

"Wyatt, it's Jax. Is Josh there?"

"No, he just went up to take a shower. He has a date tonight."

"Shit. Okay, I need a favor from you."

"What favor is that?" Apprehension moved through his mind. Jax rarely asked for anything.

"My friend, Yvette, Ette, I've spoken about her, she's in trouble and on her way to the compound. I thought we'd be back, but we've just run into a situation here and it's going to hold us up for a few hours. Can you pick her up at the airport, bring her back to the compound, show her around, and then set her up in my old room?"

"When's she coming?"

"Soon. She's flying in from Florida, I don't know much more than that, but she has a bastard for a boyfriend, hopefully, ex-boyfriend. She said she'd gotten in deep and needed help."

Wyatt took a deep breath. "How do you know she isn't bringing the trouble here?"

"I don't. It doesn't matter and you know it. We take care of those who mean something to us. When I spoke to her, she sounded scared as shit and desperate for help." Jax's voice began to take on a frustrated edge.

"I'll text you her picture and flight number as soon as I get it from her."

A quick glance at Axel and that big ass grin on his face told Wyatt he was on his own with this.

"Jax, you're going to owe me one."

"Yeah, I don't think so, Wyatt, you already owe me one. Remember the time I picked your sister up at the airport and hauled her ass around to every frigging clothing store in town until she found the perfect pair of shoes."

The laugh burst from his chest before he could stop it. "Damn that was funnier than shit, Jax."

"It wasn't. I hate shopping."

Gaining control of his laughter, he nodded. "Yeah, I got it. I'll take care of Ette for you."

"Thanks, Wyatt. I do appreciate it. We'll be back as soon as we can. Tell Axel I can hear him laughing in the background, and he's next on my list."

The line clicked off and he felt both admiration and irritation with Jax in that moment.

"Jax says you're next on her list, Axel. Her friend is coming to town so get yourself ready to have your favors called in."

Axel froze half curl, his eyebrows bunched together.

"Fuck me," he muttered, then continued to curl.

Wyatt resumed stretching his arms until the stiffness subsided.

"I'm on my way down to shoot. You coming?"

"I'll be there in a few," Axel responded.

Tossing the towel around his neck, Wyatt walked out the door and down the long hallway to the gun range. It also was situated on the first floor beneath the house. This was where all of their operations were planned, and missions were coordinated between the operatives working at the compound and the operatives assigned to working in the field. All of the vehicles were stored on the floor below. It was one of the things he loved most about living here. Everything was at the compound. Mrs. James was the main cook and housekeeper. Her daughter, Kylie, cooked for them sometimes. Together they took care of them. They had a workout facility, gun range, large computer lab and a nicely appointed medical clinic should they need it for minor types of injuries. He wasn't a surgeon, but he'd been a medic in the service and unfortunately, it came in handy in their line of work as operatives of GHOST. Life could be so much worse. He also had amassed a nice sum of money to get him through his retirement when the time came. Still, with all that was so right, he felt unsettled or maybe unhappy was the word.

Entering the outer vestibule of the gun range, he pulled his t-shirt from his back pocket and slipped it over his head. Walking to the long rack to the left, he pulled a Kevlar vest from one of the hangers and slid his arms in it. Fastening the multiple Velcro straps across his chest to secure the vest, he then turned to his locker and opened it. No need for a lock, just a place to store his practice gun and ammo.

Pulling his black textured gun case from his locker, he set it on the table to his right. Lifting the lid on his case, he once again admired his breathtaking Springfield DXM 9mm. She was a thing of beauty. She had a double stack grip and the clip held 11 rounds and one in the chamber gave him some sweet fire power.

As he pulled his gun from the solid foam holding it in place, he smiled at the weight of it in his hand. Pulling the clip from its secure resting place, he looked into it to see it fully loaded. Clicking it in place, he turned downrange, cocked the slide, and walked to the bench.

Grabbing ear plugs, he inserted them, looked at the target downrange, checked that it was 15 feet away, aimed and shot. Emptying his clip, he reloaded, inhaled the aroma of gunpowder in the air and slid the clip in place. Once more emptying his clip, he smiled as he watched his pattern on the target materialize and it was great to know he still had it.

As he removed the clip from his gun, he cocked the slide back, checked that the gun was empty, then reloaded his clip. As he pushed the last bullet into the clip, his phone buzzed in his pocket. Sliding the clip into his gun, he holstered it, then checked his phone and let out a long sigh.

3

—

... and hanging ... it was her salvation ... continued to kick and scream as loud as she could while being dragged backward by her right leg. The sidewalk bit into the skin on her knees, the left especially, her elbows, and her forearms. But damned if she'd let go of the only thing that seemed to help drag her along rather than this asshole picking her up and carrying her off because it was ...

Finally, a kick caught him in the shin, and she heard him grunt.

"Fucking bitch."

The firm hold he had on her foot loosened. She pulled her foot from his grasp, then rapidly kicked again, and landed a lucky blow in his most private of parts with the point of her heel. That was her lucky break, or so she thought. As she scrambled to her feet, the pain in her left knee caused her to intake a breath sharply which halted her for the briefest of moments. But it was enough for this monster, a depraved look in his eye, to catch his breath, and swing wildly at her, punching her in the mouth.

The searing pain that shot through her head caused her eyes to water and blood began gushing from her mouth.

Angered and scared like never before, she reached over and grabbed the extended handle of her suitcase. Mustering her strength while balancing on her heels, she lifted it and swung around landing a lucky blow to his head. She watched through her watering eyes as he hit the ground and shook his head. Through the tearing in her eyes, she could see blood dripping out of his mouth. He swiped at his face with the back of his hand and winced. Even though her eyes were blurry, the pure evil and seething anger in his look sent chills ricocheting through her body.

Spitting the blood from her mouth, she turned to run to her car and nearly tripped over her suitcase. The pain in her left knee sliced through her body, but the fear took hold and pushed her on. Her head jerked back as her attacker grabbed a handful of her hair and pulled her to him, his left hand instantly wrapped around her throat and squeezed. Letting go of her suitcase, she tried to pry his fingers from her throat while gasping for even the slightest bit of air. Dark specs started to float before her as the sunny day began to dim. As she clawed at his hand, she heard his hissing behind her, and sheer terror kept her fighting for her life. And she'd fight to the bitter end.

Hoping for one last blow, she raised her right leg, bent her knee, and kicked back at his knee as hard as she could. The crunching sound of his bone from her lucky blow reached her ears and combined with her gasp and her deep intake of breath. The deep inhalation of breath caused as much pain as the choke hold. She stumbled forward and out of his reach. Yvette bent as she faced her attacker, she'd not turn her back on him again. She picked her suitcase off the ground, stood it once again on its wheels and used it as a brace for a moment until she caught her breath and got her bearings.

Watching her attacker, she saw him as he held his leg and yelped as the pain ripped through him. His leg appeared bent at a precarious angle and she felt sure he wouldn't and, more likely, couldn't give chase any longer. But she wasn't interested in taking any further chances on that front; she'd been foolish one too many times today.

While limping to her car and swiping the blood from her chin with the neckline of her shirt, she saw her purse laying alongside her front driver side tire. Walking past it, she then turned to pick it up while she saw that her attacker wasn't following her. As she reached the driver's door, she grabbed the handle and her car unlocked. Moving to the driver side rear door, as quickly as her battered body would allow, she shoved her suitcase onto the backseat and closed the door. She eased onto the driver's seat, locked all the doors, and pushed the button on her dashboard to start the car.

When backing out of her parking spot, she glanced at the apartments across the parking lot and saw the two snotty chicks who lived across the way from her apartment. They had watched the whole thing and done nothing to help her out. Lifting her middle finger as she passed them, she let her anger take over once again. She knew as soon as the anger left and the adrenaline stopped flowing, she'd be a big puddle of tears. She needed to get to the airport, so she didn't miss her flight.

Driving out of the gates of her parking lot, she turned

left, increased her speed, and headed down the road, praying she wouldn't be followed, and she'd make it on time. She had no one here to help her and her lousy boyfriend, John Caulfield, as she'd told Jax was well-connected with local PD. The sooner she got out of this place the better, and, hopefully, what she'd just gone through was the worst that would ever happen to her. Job one when she got to Jax's was to ask Jax to teach her how to defend herself. She hated this feeling of being defenseless.

Pulling out onto the highway she gently let out a long, shaky, breath, swiped at the last remaining water in her eyes and watched the road like a hawk so there'd be no accident. As she wiped the moisture on her face, she winced when she touched her mouth and felt the blood smear. Softly touching her lips with her left hand, she could feel the swelling of her lips and forced herself not to look in the mirror. Once she got to the airport, she'd go to the restroom and clean up and change clothes before checking her bag. Just fifteen miles to go.

4

Arrive At: 4:30 ... came right after with a ... gorgeous brunette with hazel or light brown eyes. Another text after that simply said, "Ette."

Whistling softly, he shook his head and wondered what the rest of Ette looked like.

That gave him an hour and a half to shower and get to the gym. Pulling his headphones and to ease the tension, he packed his practice gun away, hung his vest, and exited the range for the elevator. The house was quiet today. They had two groups out on missions right now. Dodge, Jax, Sophie and Ford were on one mission and Lincoln and Gaige on another. He, Axel, Hawk and Josh were on rest from just completing a mission. They'd fallen into a nice routine recently. They had enough staff so that they could rest between missions. They were planning on hiring another operative, maybe two, because the work kept coming in.

Scanning his key card in front of the elevator the door

silently swished open and he stepped inside and pushed the button to the second floor. He pulled his shoulder blades back as far as he could to ease the tension that had developed while he had been in the shooting range. It wasn't the shooting that knotted him up, but the increasingly frequent thoughts about Dany, his daughter. What was she, 18 now? When was the last time he saw her? It had to have been five years. Tomorrow was her birthday, which he knew was why his thoughts floated to her so often. But last year when he tried calling her, she refused to take his call. He couldn't blame her; she barely knew him.

The elevator door slid open and he stepped off and into the hallway on the second floor where their rooms were located. Gaige and Sophie's suite was all the way at the end of the hall to the right. Hawk and Roxanne's rooms at the end of the hallway to the left. Axel's room was across from his, Jax's next to Axel's and Josh's on the opposite side of the stairs to the right. His room was to the left, just before Hawk and Roxanne's rooms. He turned left and admired the open staircase to the grand foyer where Jax and Dodge had been married just a few months ago. In just a week, Gaige and Sophie were getting married here as well. It made a perfect setting for a wedding. Plus, they were all protected here. And the convenience of the underground bunker, shooting range, workout facility, command center, parking garage and clinic made this place perfect for all of their needs.

Pushing the handle down to open his door he inhaled deeply as the sanctuary within a sanctuary surrounded him. The coloring suited him. The walls were a deep gray; the furniture was black leather, at least his sofa and recliner were. The coffee table was an old piece of wooden furniture he had years ago when he had been married. His sister had painted it a cream color for him years ago and he just couldn't part with it. The carpeting was gray, a lighter shade than the walls. Roxanne had teased him about how cold it felt to her when she'd seen it for the first time, but it made him feel at home.

He pulled his t-shirt off as he walked through the sitting area to the bedroom. Tossing it into the basket in the corner, which he used for his hamper, he opened the top drawer of his dresser and pulled fresh underwear and socks from inside. The second drawer held his t-shirts, mostly black; he grabbed the first one on top and closed the drawer. Walking into the bathroom, he reached into the glass walled shower and twisted the faucet to warm the water while he retrieved a clean pair of tactical pants from his closet.

The room began to steam from the hot water. He rotated his head to the left three times, then slowly to the right. Tomorrow, he'd call Dany and wish her a happy birthday even if he had to leave it on a voicemail. He'd at least try to communicate with her.

After finishing his shower and dressing, he tucked his keys into his front pocket, his wallet in his back right pocket and his phone next to his left leg in its hidden pocket and his gun in the right hidden pocket. Gawd, he loved his tactical pants. Exiting his room, he turned to the right and walked the few steps down the hall to the grand staircase and turned to take the steps down to the main level. His knee had been good for some time now and it remained that way as long as he took care of it with just enough exercise. Once in a while he still had to ice it, but overall, he was still spry, able to run when he had to and perform the necessary tasks as an operative.

At the bottom of the steps he turned right and walked under the balcony and to the kitchen in the back. He pocketed two meal bars from the basket, inhaled the aroma of something in the oven, and wondered where Mrs. James was. Not seeing anyone around he shrugged, grabbed a bottle of water from the refrigerator, and headed to the elevator and the garage below ground.

***

Wyatt walked up to the digital board in the airport for the third time, glanced again at the picture of Yvette on his phone and looked around the large area as the passengers exited the plane. He didn't see anyone who looked like Yvette, not even close. Finally, another passenger walked through the door from the plane and what he saw made him wince. A battered woman with a swollen mouth, bruised around her left temple, wearing loose fitting blue pants, the kind that looked like they could be a skirt, too, and a long-sleeved loose-fitting brown top, limped along. She stopped and pulled her phone from the purse that hung from her left shoulder, tapped a few times and looked around. She sent off a text or message of some sort, then looked around the room again. His phone chimed that he got a text and he looked down to see a message from Jax. "Ette just got off the plane."

Swallowing he slowly approached the beaten woman, his heart hurt for her ailments and the scared look in her eyes. As he neared, he said, "Yvette?"

She backed away from him, fear clear on her face. He held his hands up as if to show her he meant no harm.

"I'm Wyatt. Jax sent me. She's stuck on a mission."

She swallowed then looked down at the phone she was holding as if it were her lifeline. Then it pinged and she read the message she'd just gotten.

Her eyes met his again and he nodded.

"I won't hurt you, honestly. I'm friendly."

He stood perfectly still because he was afraid she'd bolt. The look of pure terror on her face, which he knew was beautiful, but now was battered and bruised made him sad. It also pissed him off that some asshole would hit on a woman. Any woman. It was out and out bullshit.

5

Literally not only was Jax not here to ... from the airport, she sent a gigantic man with tattoos up both arms and on his hands. A scar parted his beard on his left cheek, and it looked like it was a nasty scar that ran down to his neck. He looked dangerous and deadly. That's what she'd just run away from. So, what the hell?

Her ... she'd ... for ... fine. Her face hurt and every time she moved her jaw to talk it throbbed like hell. Her elbows pounded with each heartbeat but not as much as her head. She needed aspirin, water, and a bed. But first she needed to bandage up her knees and elbows. She'd been able to clean them up a little after she arrived at the Florida airport. When she was in the restroom, she used wet paper towels and water. She didn't have antibiotic ointment or bandages to apply to her knees and elbows before changing her clothes. While she was on the plane to Indiana, she felt that her elbows had bled, and her long sleeves stuck to them. Likewise, the loose-fitting pants she wore stuck to her knees, too.

She looked up at this big man, and his amber-colored eyes looked almost as if they were pleading with her. He was probably afraid she'd burst into tears. If he only knew how close she was to doing just that, he'd turn and run. Men hated when women cried. Most men did, not John, that bastard.

"Hey, it's okay, I promise."

She looked at her phone again and reread the text message from Jax. "Stuck on a mission. I'm sorry. I've sent Wyatt to pick you up. He'll get you to the compound and set you up in my old room until I get back. He's a gentleman."

She swallowed the lump in her throat, then asked him, "What's your name again?"

"Wyatt."

"How do I know you're really Wyatt?"

He nodded his head once, then pulled his wallet from his back pocket. Opening it he pulled out two cards and handed them to her. She tried to keep her hands from shaking but was unsuccessful. She took the cards and looked closely at them; one of them was his driver's license, which stated Wyatt Lawson, 6'7" in height, 239 lbs., Black hair, Amber eyes. The picture was the man standing before her. The second card was identifying him as an operative with GHOST. Same identifying information as his driver's license.

Huffing out a long breath she handed his cards back to him then raised her phone and snapped his picture. Quickly adding it to a text she sent to Jax, "Is this Wyatt?"

Jax responded quickly enough. "Yes."

Nodding she tucked her phone into her purse, looked at Wyatt and said, "Thank you for picking me up."

She winced when she tried to smile and realized it undoubtedly looked rather odd as the swollen side of her face didn't seem to move.

"How badly are you injured? I can get a wheelchair to get you to the baggage claim. It's a journey."

Shaking her head, she stepped forward, winced again and, he said, "Please, let's get a wheelchair and make this easier on both of us. When we get back to the compound, I'll take a look at your wounds and make sure you don't need to seek a doctor's help."

"How would you know that?"

"I'm a medic, Yvette."

He motioned for her to sit in one of the chairs in the boarding area. Then he held out his hand for support if she needed it. Her mind wrestled with wanting to take his hand and then not wanting to. She was a hot mess right now. In the end she lay her hand in his and his strength almost made her cry as he solicitously helped her to a chair.

"I'll be right back."

He looked into her eyes waiting for her to respond so she nodded her head. He took a step then halted.

"Seriously, you're not going to run, are you? Jax will kill me if I lose you."

The fact that this big man was afraid of Jax told her everything she needed to know. Jax was fierce and she'd been right in calling her for help.

She laughed then winced and held the left side of her face.

"I'll be right back."

This time he disappeared down the corridor in search

of a wheelchair. She pulled her purse to her lap and wrapped her hands around it as if it were precious cargo. Actually, at this moment in time it was all she had. Everything else was in her suitcase and she felt a building need to get to it as soon as possible. Hopefully, Wyatt would be back soon before she cried or panicked. Maybe both.

Trying not to be obvious she continued to watch in the direction Wyatt had disappeared to praying it wouldn't be long before he returned. Her iron grip on her purse was her lifeline at this point. Glancing ahead she saw a man staring at her and it sent a wild chill down her spine. She stood trying to seem as though nothing was wrong. What if John had called someone here to intercept her? She couldn't sit and wait around. She needed to get to her suitcase then hide somewhere until Jax came.

Rounding the corner, she limped down the corridor searching the signs for the direction to the baggage claim. By now her suitcase might be on the carousel, what if someone took it? Her breathing rapidly increased, and the panic she'd been so successful restraining suddenly seized her. She limped as fast as she could, her knees throbbed with each movement, but she couldn't stop. Not now.

Finally, seeing a sign for the baggage claim it showed that she needed to go downstairs. Sending up a silent prayer that there was an escalator she was halted by a hand on her shoulder.

"Where do you think you're going?"

6

———

... those gorgeous ... stared back at him. He saw ... process who he was and that he wasn't a threat. She blinked several times and then cried out a groan of relief when she saw him.

"Hey, you said you'd wait," he said while trying not to scare her.

"I couldn't. There was a man staring at me. I thought maybe I knew ... him to kill me. I couldn't wait."

"Okay. So, sit down in this chair and let me get you to baggage, then we'll go back to the compound where you'll be completely safe."

She stared at him for a long time at least it felt like a long time. He saw her shoulders relax slightly, then she swallowed. Finally, she looked down at the wheelchair next to him and her shoulders relaxed further. It probably looked like a golden chariot at that point by the way she reacted. He'd watched her limp along and knew she was in pain.

She limped toward him in three steps while he walked

behind the chair and held it in place for her. She sat down and pulled her purse in front of her body and wrapped both arms around it hugging it close to her.

Kneeling in front of her chair, he pulled the footrests down, and gently lifted her feet, one at a time, onto their respective footrests. He caught her gaze in his, and smiling said, "Ready?"

Moisture gathered in her eyes and he braced himself for a flood of tears, but they didn't come. She simply nodded at him and swallowed again, and then pulled her arms tighter around her purse. He knew it was time to get her suitcase and then next to the Beast so she could begin to feel secure once more. Hopefully, it wouldn't be long before he could find out what she'd gone through, but realistically that just might have to wait until Jax got back. With any luck that wouldn't be long.

Successfully navigating the crowds and making it to the baggage area, he watched for the signs that would lead them to the carousel her bag was likely now circling. Hoping to stave off a breakdown, he lightly lay his hand on her shoulder and leaned down whispering in her ear, "Don't worry, Yvette. I don't think the luggage has come down yet, see all those people waiting. We're good."

He found the correct carousel but there weren't any bags on the carousel, and he heard her sharp intake of breath.

A loud beeping sounded three times above them and the carousel began moving. He squeezed her shoulder gingerly and said, "When you see your bag tell me which it is, and I'll grab it for you."

Her voice was soft when she responded, "Okay."

He patiently waited as the luggage fell from the conveyor and people quickly jostled each other to grab their bags and get out of there. Happy for the clearing of some of the crowd he glanced down at Yvette only to find her staring as if she were looking for her salvation.

" There it's right there the blue one."

"Got it."

He squeezed her shoulder again then easily reached her suitcase, lifted it off the carousel, and set it on its wheels. Turning he began wheeling it to her and he saw the tears that streamed down her cheeks. Just tears, no other crying sounds and it broke his heart for what this woman must have just gone through.

He situated her suitcase between him and her wheelchair, then slowly began pushing both along the corridors to get them to the Beast. It was a slow process as sometimes his steps became out of sync with the suitcase, but he made it finally to the parking lot.

"Do you want to wait here for me to bring the Beast to you or do you want me to wheel you to the Beast?"

"The Beast?"

"It's one of our vehicles. It's up to you, either is fine with me, Yvette."

"I'd prefer to go with you. But we can leave the chair here, I can walk."

"You sure?"

"Yeah."

She slowly lifted the footrests with the tops of her feet, and he held the chair firmly as she scooted forward, then stood. Allowing her to regain her balance he stood still until she turned and nodded at him.

Maneuvering the chair back, he was grateful a porter came along. The porter asked if it was an airport chair, and, if so, was he finished with the chair, which was clearly airport property as evident by the stamped name on the back of the chair.

"Yes, thank you."

He reached into his wallet and pulled a five-dollar bill out and handed it to the porter who smiled broadly and backed away with the chair.

Taking Yvette's suitcase in his left hand, he held his right arm out to her and was grateful when she wrapped her left arm through his right and leaned a bit of her weight onto him.

"We'll go slow and when you need a break you just say so."

"Okay."

He guessed her height at about 5'6" or so. Slender in form, he could tell she had strength in her. After the beat-down she had taken today and had kept going told him she had the mental fortitude to eventually be fine.

Seeing the Beast up ahead, he pointed to it and said, "We're almost there."

She kept limping along and after a few steps, she said, "I see why you call it the Beast."

Chuckling, he said, "You haven't seen the half of it."

Pulling the key fob from his pocket he unlocked the Beast and had the liftgate opening as they reached it. He stopped at the back end and Yvette let go of his arm as he lifted her suitcase and set it in the back. Pushing a button on the bottom of the gate, he slowly led her around to the front passenger side door, opened it for her, and held his arm out again for her as she climbed in. It didn't take nearly as long as he feared. Her confidence in him and her positive situation must be coming to her. She knew she was secure. That was a good sign indeed.

He closed her door, walked around the front of the Beast, and climbed into the driver's seat.

"It's about a forty-minute drive. If you feel like you need to rest, please go ahead. I promise you you're safe now."

She tried to smile again, then winced, and whispered, "Thank you."

Now, he just had to get them back to the compound and see about her wounds.

the driveway which ... at the top of the incline ... ornate black wrought-iron gates came into view. Wyatt rolled down his window, waved his security card, and the gates silently slid open. Driving around a corner there stood an enormous, beautiful, Southern Mansion style home complete with an expansive covered front porch. Rather than driving up to the front door, Wyatt parked in front of the garage doors, waving his card once again at the garage panel, the door lifted. Entering the garage, the drive sent them down to below the compound. She gasped as they began driving underground. She'd never have guessed looking at the home there was anything underground.

He chuckled, "Sorry, I should have warned you. The garage is two levels below the compound."

"Wow. I had no idea. Jax has mentioned the compound, but for some reason I pictured a bunker or barracks looking place, austere and ugly."

"Yeah, Gaige insisted that if we all had to live together

it would be nice as well as functional. Plus, he didn't want anyone to ever suspect that this mansion was GHOST's Headquarters. Before living here, we were in North Carolina. While it wasn't as nice as this, it accommodated each of us and worked well as GHOST Headquarters. This was remodeled with all of our needs in mind after the needs of GHOST."

He turned left, then left again, then left one more time as they descended further below ground. It was all well-lit, clean, and painted white. Finally reaching the garage she saw neatly lined cars, trucks, and motorcycles, all at an angle, all spotless and relatively new. There were a few empty spaces here and there, which was understandable.

"So, we each have two assigned spaces for parking. It keeps bickering to a minimum, which actually isn't an issue at all. While we can each bust each other's balls here and there, we're fortunate in that we all get along. It's one of the main things we look at when bringing new members on board."

He drove past a few of the cars, then continued, "That's my black Corvette and a copper Ram pickup truck. Jax's Jeep is right there, her bike is at home."

She laughed remembering Jax bitching about the first time she met Dodge. The swelling on her face tugged and her jaw hurt. Her left hand instinctively flew to hold her face.

Dropping her hand to her lap, she explained, "I remember Jax telling me about the first time she met Dodge. Sort of rocky in the beginning."

Wyatt chuckled and she turned her head to see his smile. She'd like to see his face without the beard. His smile was gorgeous, and his dimples made his scar less intimidating. He had unusual eyes, a bit like hers, more amber than brown and a little cat like. With his long, black hair they reminded her of amber tiger eyes. She suspected he wore his hair long, in part, to cover his scar.

"Yes, Jax was madder than a wet cat when the bounty hunters walked into the room and she saw Dodge. She was so angry because she thought he'd interfered with her mission the night before. He had a different version of the story. It all worked out in the end though."

She simply nodded.

He pulled the vehicle, the Beast, into a parking spot and put it in park.

"So, you and Jax went to high school together?"

"Yeah, in North Carolina, then right after graduation, my family moved to Florida, but we stayed close. She was fierce, even then. Nobody bothered Jax in school, 'cause she'd kick their ass. I was always grateful that she was my friend. When she's your friend, she's loyal, when she's not your friend, she can be a pain in the ass."

He chuckled and nodded.

"Okay, so we'll go up in the elevator. Jax asked that I show you around but what I'd really like to do is check you out."

"What?"

He shook his head and winced.

"Sorry, that didn't come out right." He twisted a bit in the driver's seat. "I'm a medic, remember. And we have a small clinic here so, I want to clean and treat your wounds and bandage them; and then I'll make sure you don't have anything broken."

Her shoulders relaxed and then her cheeks flamed hot. She felt silly about her assumption and for forgetting he'd told her that earlier.

"I'm sorry." She shook her head slightly. "I'm not myself at all today."

"Understandable. Are you ready to head up to the clinic?"

"Yeah." She unbuckled her seatbelt. Then she pulled her purse strap over her shoulder while Wyatt jumped from the custom-made SUV and walked around the front of it to her door. He opened it and held his right hand out to assist her.

"Take your time we're in no hurry."

"Thanks."

She slowly turned in her seat and set her feet on the running board of the Beast. Scooting to the edge of the seat, she grabbed his right hand, and straightened her right leg to step down. When her left knee burned as she bent it, she halted, put her right leg up on the running board and stretched her left leg out to step down on that one.

He was a fantastic support system. He didn't get inpatient with her.

After she had finally stepped down from the Beast, she halted for a moment.

"I'm sorry, sitting for a bit stiffened up my knees and elbows."

"Understandable. You likely have swelling and dried blood as well. After we get you cleaned up, we'll put antibiotic salve and bandages on your wounds, then give you something for the pain and swelling. You'll feel better before Jax gets home. Mrs. James will probably have dinner ready for us soon. Whatever she's making, it smelled amazing when I left. So, something in your stomach will help to nourish you and make you feel better, too."

"Who's Mrs. James?"

"She and her daughter, Kylie, cook and clean for us. Mrs. James does most of the cooking and housekeeping."

"Wow. You all must live a great life."

He chuckled and she liked how he sounded when he did. "When we aren't dodging bullets it's great."

"Right."

She felt foolish for about the third or fourth time in a few minutes and she hated feeling that way. After a nap she'd hopefully feel better and not sound so asinine. And maybe Jax would be home soon.

They slowly walked to the back of the SUV where Wyatt stopped her, let go of her left hand, and opened the back to pull her suitcase out. Then, setting it on its wheels, he pushed the button on the bottom of the liftgate and it began to close. Holding his right arm out once again for her, she slid her hand into the crook of it and used his strength to walk to the elevator.

He waved his card in front of a panel on the elevator and the doors quietly slid open. He let her limp in first, then he followed with her suitcase and touched the button that read Conf.

"It's going to be okay, Yvette, I promise."

"Thank you, I hope you're right."

8

____

... didn't know what ... to make her comfortable. It ... that she was scared as a new puppy. She had her purse hung over her shoulder, but she had pulled it in front of her and clung onto it with both hands. It was as if her purse could magically transport her somewhere safe if things went south.

But he had to admit, she was smart. She looked at everything. He saw as around the elevator as if she were memorizing everything in case she needed to run.

The elevator slowed and the doors whooshed open revealing the conference room level of the compound. She made no attempt to move, so he held his hand out before him and said, "After you."

He saw her lips twitch as if she meant to smile then stopped presumably because it hurt. She walked out ahead of him and waited for directions.

"To the left and down the hall to the end."

She slowly walked as she looked at the newly hung paintings on the walls, which mirrored the upstairs with famous battle scenes in American history, Generals and military heroes.

The frosted glass door to the clinic was closed and she stopped just in front of it. Leaning forward he pulled down on the handle and pushed it open.

Yvette stepped into the clinic and the lights automatically turned on illuminating the pristine room. He and Gaige prided themselves on the state of this room always. For some reason he wanted her to be impressed with it.

She whispered, "Wow." And his chest swelled.

He skirted around her and rolled her suitcase to stand against the wall to his left. He patted the padded table in the center of the room.

"Sit up here. Do you need help?"

Her cheeks flushed pink and he thought she'd look lovely once she healed.

"I think I can manage."

He washed his hands and then began preparing sterile gauze and warm water to clean her wounds. He gathered antibacterial ointments in individual foil packets to dress them, non-stick gauze pads to bandage them, and ibuprofen for pain and placed them on a wheeled tray. Pulling rubber gloves out of a box he slipped them on his hands. Turning to make sure she'd situated herself on the table he met her eyes as she watched him prepare for her.

"I won't cause you any pain."

She swallowed but nodded.

Walking to the mini fridge in the corner, he pulled out a bottle of water and an ice pack and set them on the tray.

Wheeling the tray to the table she sat on, he pulled up a stool from the opposite side of the room and sat in front of her knees. Handing her the bottle of water and the little paper cup with the ibuprofen, he waited until she took them from him.

"Ibuprofen for the swelling and the pain. The water is self-explanatory." He smiled and looked her in the eyes. What he didn't expect was his heart to beat faster when she met his eyes with hers and held. She swallowed and he wasn't sure what he waited for. Then she tipped the cup back against her lips and dropped the ibuprofen into her mouth, unscrewed the plastic cap from the water and took a long drink. Putting the cap back on the water, she then held the cold bottle to the left side of her swollen face and closed her eyes.

"Let's start with your knees and then we'll take a look at your elbows."

"How did you know my elbows were..."

"You've bled onto your shirt."

She turned her arms downward and looked at the blood spots that had seeped through.

"You must think I'm a frigging mess."

"No, I think you're a woman who was beaten today and is lucky it wasn't so much worse."

Quietly she said, "Yeah."

The material of her loose-fitting pants was stuck to her knees, so he wet gauze pads in the warm water and held it over the material on them to soften the blood. She twitched slightly but made no other moves.

"What do you do for a living?"

She inhaled and said, "I'm a manager in the customer service department for a large corporation, JAS Enterprises."

Looking down at his hands on her knees, she continued, "I was anyway. I won't be able to go back there."

"Why not?"

"My boyfri..." She stopped and swallowed. "My ex is well-connected there, and I was lucky, as you've mentioned, to be alive. What you see is only after the result of me fighting like hell and landing a lucky mule kick to my attacker's knee. Last I saw of him his knee looked much worse than either of mine and was bent at a precarious angle."

That was the most she'd said since he'd met her, and he felt it was a good sign.

"Wanna tell me about it?"

The door burst open and a storm named Jax rushed in.

"Where the hell have you..." Jax looked at his hands on Yvette's now bare legs, her pant legs rolled up, her knees scraped up and some of the skin rubbed completely off of them. "What the hell happened to you? Did that son of a bitch do this to you?"

He looked up at Jax to make sure she wasn't talking about him, but she was looking at Yvette.

"No. He sent one of his men."

"One of his me..." Jax walked forward and wrapped her arms around Yvette's shoulders. "You need to tell me what's going on and now."

The tears started falling when she saw Jax, which was his cue to keep working. He couldn't deal with women crying. And Yvette had been so stoic since he first saw her battered face. Had been a rock in his mind.

His heart pounded wildly because there was too much estrogen in this room now. He pushed his stool away from the table. Jax immediately replaced him in that spot and held Yvette to her shoulder.

9

[...] so good. Her [...] she'd held back [...] to get out of her at once. More sobs broke from her throat and she cried into Jax's strong shoulder. Jax's arms hugged her tighter but she said nothing; Jax was just there letting her know she was safe.

Finally, her tears subsided, and she pulled away. Swiping under her right eye she sniffed loudly and was surprised when Wyatt stepped closer in with two tissues held out to her. Dabbing at her left eye, which hurt where she touched the bruising, she carefully cleaned her face up, then gently blew her nose.

Jax walked to a wastebasket against the wall close to the door and brought it over. Dropping the used tissues into the basket, she watched as Jax's gorgeous, but sharp eyes assessed her.

"Tell me...us what happened."

Clearing her throat, she watched with fascination as Wyatt stepped forward. Without a word, Jax stepped aside and let him take his place in front of her again. He eyes drifted down to watch Wyatt working on her knees and she saw Jax's jaw twitch as she clenched her teeth together then relaxed.

"I suspected something was off for a while now. I tried breaking up with John a couple of months ago because, frankly, he became increasingly violent and I wanted nothing to do with that. But recently he's been more agitated than ever, and I heard some words that disturbed the hell out of me."

Jax stood close and alternated between watching Wyatt and her.

"What words?"

"RICO. As in investigation."

Wyatt's hands stopped adding salve to her knees as he looked up at her.

"What has he been doing that would prompt a RICO investigation?"

She swallowed because honestly she felt stupid that she didn't see it before.

Tucking her hair behind her right ear, she closed her eyes and took in a deep breath.

"I think he's been involved in a kidnapping."

Wyatt's back straightened and he inhaled deeply then let it out slowly. Turning his head, he looked at Jax. His brows raised and she nodded once.

"Ette? It's unlikely that a RICO investigation would be initiated over one kidnapping. I think we need to start at the beginning. Let's go back to why you wanted to break up with him a few months ago."

Clearing her throat lightly she squared her shoulders. "We went out to eat. He liked going to this hotel, the Bismark."

She paused but neither Wyatt nor Jax said anything, so she continued.

"Anyway, I never felt very comfortable there, but he insisted. There was a girl sitting at the bar alone. She looked young, maybe drinking age. Dressed to the nines, to be honest, she looked desperate to me, dress too short, heels too high, makeup overdone, hair too blond, you know, like she was trolling or something. John kept looking at her, which was irritating me, but then again, not all that much because I knew it was over for me. What irritated me was that I was sitting right there, and it was frigging rude."

"He's an asshole," Jax spat out.

"He is." She glanced at Wyatt who remained sitting on his stool, but he was listening and looking at her, which startled her a bit. His eyes were almost cat-like. An amber color she'd never seen in any person. Framed by his black hair and close-cut beard, he was breathtaking.

"So, I thought that would be a good time to tell him I was finished with him. He could move on to Miss Desperate and it would be easy for me to leave. But before I could say the words, he leaned over and said, 'Go over and chat with her.' "I said, 'excuse me?' And he repeated go over and chat with her. I told him fuck off. "

Her eyes darted to Wyatt's then to Jax. Their expressions were complete opposites. Jax smiled ear to ear. Wyatt's brows furrowed.

"Then he grabbed my arm and twisted it slightly and dropped his voice to a low growl almost. And he said again, 'I said, go fucking chat with her. Now.'"

Rubbing her palms together slowly to dispel some of her nervousness she paused.

Jax lay her left hand over her hands and two things

struck her. She was behaving as if she were guilty of something and Jax had the prettiest wedding and engagement rings she'd ever seen. She stared at the glittering pink diamond, then looked into her friend's gorgeous eyes.

"Your rings are gorgeous, Jax, totally unique."

Jax positively glowed. There was something about her appearance. It was like she sparkled or, nope, glowed was the right word. She glowed.

"Right? Dodge did good. I'll tell you all about how he came to get a hold of this diamond later on. It's the story of how we met in many ways."

Wyatt laughed out loud and shook his head. Raising his hand, thumb pointed at Jax he said, "I heard she was so pissed off that she had to work with Dodge the first gig out. Everyone at the compound waited for them to return. They thought she'd kill him."

Jax shoved his shoulder. "Shut up."

"Ette, tell us what happened."

"I got up and walked to the bar and sat down next to the blond. I asked her what her name was, and she told me Lola. So, I made small talk. I looked back at John a few times and he was texting and watching us. About ten minutes later, John walked over to us and told me it was time to go. He paid for Lola's drink, nodded to the bartender, and we left. As we were leaving the Bismark, one of John's men walked in and John whispered to him, 'Bar.' He grabbed me by the arm and jerked me to the car."

Anyway, a couple of days later I saw a news report on the television about that girl, Lola. Her hair was dark though, but it sure looked like her. The report said she'd been missing for two days. John stormed into the room, turned the TV off, and bitched at me for watching it.

"I grabbed my purse and told him it was time to part

ways, that I was tired of his shitty behavior, and I left. That day flowers showed up at work and at home. He knocked on my door one evening with a bouquet of roses in his hand, and the second he came through the door he said he was sorry and to give him another chance."

particularly

shredded in places,

were needed.

"You'll probably have a scar here on your left knee, but there's nothing to do about it. It'll get you street cred."

Jax laughed. Yvette just nodded. "Guess that can come in handy. I can always raise my pant leg and say, 'You want a piece of this?' That will have them running for sure."

He smiled. He both laughed, and he realized her sense of humor was beginning to come back. Feeling safe had a way of doing that.

He stood then. "Now I need to look at your elbows."

Yvette nodded and lifted one sleeve up carefully. He held a hand up to her to halt her progress.

Wyatt said, "The blood has dried, and your shirt is sticking to your elbow."

Dabbing a fresh gauze pad in the warm water, he gently held it over her shirt on her elbow to soften the hardened blood. Checking often and as soon as he could move the fabric from her wound, he nodded to her. She moved her other sleeve up her arm slowly. He wet another gauze pad and handed it to Jax, who took it without a word and mimicked his actions on her other arm. They'd done this a few times over the years. All of the GHOST operatives were assistants to Gaige or him when the time called for them to be.

Jax interrupted the silence. "So, you took him back?"

Yvette's shoulders straightened then she whispered, "Yeah."

Jax, to her credit, didn't berate her or make her feel bad, she just nodded. He glanced over Yvette's head to see Jax's expression though; it was clear on her face that she was frustrated that her friend had gone back to that asshole.

"Tell us more, Ette."

"So, we went on a date to a movie. And then the following week he was out of town for work. But when he came back, he wanted to go back to the Bismark. I told him I didn't want to go, and he said he had a surprise for me. So, he enticed me into going. When we got there, we sat at our table, which was always the same table in the corner. It enabled him to watch the door, which he always did. I asked him where my surprise was. He looked taken off guard and said he'd forgotten to bring it. I knew then there was no surprise. Sometimes, like that night, I wondered why he even wanted me at the hotel. But we sat there pretending to look at the menu. I was not interested in being there and wondered what was wrong with me that I'd gotten back with him. I felt dirty in some way. I was also a little afraid of him and not sure how to actually break it off permanently." Yvette looked up at Jax and said, "Pretty lame, right?"

Jax shook her head, "No, not at all. Battered women

always go through this. And, while he didn't hit you, he man-handled you and made you feel scared. Unsure. Not yourself. That's what they do. They take away who you are so you don't have any confidence in yourself and will do what they say. It's mental abuse and as bad as physical abuse."

Yvette took a deep breath and he felt so bad for her. Applying antibiotic salve to her elbow, he gently bandaged her up then moved to the other side. Jax quietly dropped the soiled gauze pad she'd held to Yvette's elbow into the wastebasket still sitting alongside Yvette and moved to the other side of the table.

"Anyway," Yvette continued. "The night played out the same way. He watched a younger brunette walk into the bar and sit down. This time I noticed the bartender nod at John, and John began texting someone. The brunette looked around like she was uncomfortable and about to leave when John told me to go and chat with her. I asked him why and the stare he leveled on me sent chills down my spine. At that point, I knew he was up to something horrible. And he was using me to do it. So, rather than leave this time like I wanted to, I decided to see if I could find out what he was up to."

Jax shook her head, "Ette, you may have put yourself in a lot of danger. If this beating you took is any indication, you absolutely did."

"I know that now. But I had to know what he was doing."

Wyatt inserted himself into the conversation. "What is he doing, Yvette?"

She turned to him. Her tawny-brown eyes against her brunette mane with the red highlights running through it was striking. Even with a swollen bruised face. "At first I thought it was prostitution. Finding these young women and locking them up somewhere to turn tricks. What I couldn't understand was why he used me. Pimps have been doing this for years and these girls looked like they were already turning tricks or about too or just looking for a sugar daddy. Still, why didn't he just approach them himself?"

Not able to look away from her eyes, her sad expression called to him in some way. "He was involving you, so you were an accomplice. To keep you in line."

He watched her swallow and her eyes welled with moisture, but tears didn't fall. Blinking rapidly, she kept them to herself.

"So, if not prostitution what then?" he asked.

"Trafficking. I found out just before I left today. I figured out how to hack into his email account. I lifted his username and password while he was in the shower yesterday. At home, once I knew he'd left town this morning, I logged into his account and found emails about some transactions of money, large sums of money, being deposited into a few bank accounts one was international. In all instances, it was two days after each of these women had been in the bar at the Bismark."

"How did he find out you figured it out?"

Jax's posture stiffened but Yvette continued to look at him. "He must have a trace on anyone logging into his email account. I hadn't been in it more than five minutes and he texted me and said 'You keep your fucking mouth shut or I'll shut it for you.' About an hour later, he sent another text that said something like the first second I see you, I'm going to kill you, you little snitch."

She turned away from him then and looked at Jax. "I called the airport and made a reservation and then called you. I was throwing things into a suitcase as I had you on the phone."

He straightened his posture as a chill ran through him. "Do you still have your cell phone?"

"Yes."

"We need it, Yvette, he could use it to track you. He likely hid a device or app in your phone when you weren't aware so he could find you.

"Do you still have his phone?" Jax asked.

"We should be able to trace his phone with our tech and connections."

"Oh my God, I am so stupid. I never thought of that."

She reached behind her for her purse and opened the zippered top. Reaching inside she pulled her cell phone out, and Jax immediately took it from her, held it up to her face, her fingerprint, then scrolled to the contacts.

Jax promptly went to the texts sent from John today. Then she scrolled through her phone while Wyatt finished cleaning up her second elbow. His hands were soothing as he dabbed at the blood and scrapes on her elbow. His fingers were adept at their task. His warmth seeped into her when he brushed her arms and she'd be lying if she said she didn't like it.

Jax pulled her own phone from her back pocket and scrolled with her thumb, then stopped, tapped on an icon, and held her phone to Yvette's. Jax's phone beeped and she read the screen.

Turning her phone to her, Jax asked, "Do you play this game?"

She shook her head, "No, I didn't even know it was on there."

She saw the look that passed between Jax and Wyatt and she wanted to cry. "He's been tracking me."

"Yes. I'll run this over to Gaige and ask him to do an analysis on it. Maybe he can locate, find and remove the information that John has been gathering. Then we'll have to shut it down and pull the battery. I'll get you a new phone."

Her heart throbbed faster, and her stomach felt as if she'd swallowed a rock. That rock somehow felt like it was on fire as she thought about all the things John knew about her, especially where she was.

Glancing at Jax's retreating back she swallowed once again, and Wyatt's hand softly wrapped around her fore-arm. "Don't worry, no one can get to you here. We have more security than Fort Knox."

Turning to look at him, she saw some things she hadn't noticed before. He had fine lines around his eyes that told of a life lived. His eyes were a beautiful color with specks of gold in the amber. While she had unusually colored eyes herself, a light brown that looked tawny, his were so much more mesmerizing. But there was something else in his eyes that she noticed and that was a sort of sadness.

"Thank you, but I can't stay here forever."

He paused and stared into her eyes then continued applying the antibacterial ointment to her elbow without saying anything further.

"Okay, I'm finished. If you like I'll show you to Jax's old room and you can unpack, wash up, and change clothes if you want. Mrs. James will be able to get that blood out of your blouse and pants."

"Are you sure?"

"Believe me, she's had plenty of practice with us. She's a master at it."

Her tummy flipped, "That makes me feel so sad, but I've got clothes in my suitcase from earlier today that is loaded with blood."

"Okay, we'll take it to her and see what she can do, but she's got mad laundry skills. I think you'll be surprised."

She thought for a moment, then asked, "Is what you all do that dangerous?"

He pulled his rubber gloves off as he stared at her. Dropping the gloves into the wastebasket he finally responded. "Has Jax shared much with you about what we do?"

Shaking her head, she replied, "Just that she helps remove scum from the streets. Not a lot else. I assumed she was working with the police or something." Waving her hand around as if encompassing the room, 'I had no idea she lived like this. In a place like this. Or used to. I'm actually dumbfounded about all of this and have been trying to process everything, but I simply can't right now."

He crossed his arms in front of him and she knew that was an invisible barrier of sorts. Protective. He continued to stare at her as if trying to figure out how much to tell her.

"How tall are you?" It flew from her mouth before she could think about it. But he towered over her and Jax, too. Yet, he was sensitive. Like a big bear or something.

He chuckled and his face transformed into something stunning. His long dark hair, and beard framed a face she assumed was classic Norseman. Like the Vikings she'd seen on television or in the movies. Strong features built solid and sturdy, and able to handle themselves. That's what he reminded her of Vikings except for his black hair and unusual amber eyes. He grinned again and his dimples emphasized his smile but also the scar on the left side of his face. She saw the hair on his beard part and the scar that ran the length of the left side of his face and neck and curved behind it.

"Where did that come from?" He asked.

She could feel the blush as it crawled up her chest and to her cheeks. "I don't know. I guess my senses are returning. I can't help but notice that you are likely the tallest man I've ever seen."

He laughed. "You haven't met Hawk yet. He's an inch taller at 6'8."

Her eyes rounded and he laughed again.

"I'd like to know what you all do here. That is if you can tell me."

He moved to stand in front of her, then pulled up his stool and sat down, which nearly brought him to eye level.

"I can tell you this much. We work largely for the government. Sometimes we take private clients but mostly the government. We go on missions, which usually involve rescue and sometimes recon. We step in where the military and local law enforcement can't go because of laws and restrictions. We, in a sense, fill in the gap."

"Is it dangerous?"

"Often."

She nodded and swallowed to moisten her parched throat. And a bit of sadness, for some reason. "That means Jax is in danger a lot?"

He laughed then and it was beautiful and spontaneous. "Jax is one tough ass chick. She can hold her own. Ask her about saving Dodge's life."

"No way, she saved his life?" She laughed and even though her face was swollen and hurt a bit, it felt good to laugh.

"Yep. He got shot in the shoulder and she had to help get him out of harm's way. Then she had to cover him while I went to get the Beast so we could get him to the hospital. I did what I could applying pressure to try to stop the bleeding. It wasn't stopping so, she applied pressure while I drove like a bat out of hell to get him to the local hospital."

"Oh, my God. I'll make sure to ask her about it."

Jax walked into the room, her jaw tight, her posture stiff. "He's been tracking you for a while, Ette. You're going to need to stay here where it's safe. Our house is fairly secure, but there are more people here and better security. Wyatt will help you navigate the place and I'll come every day."

12

———

[illegible] when the [illegible] seen the picture Jax [illegible] so he knew who he was looking for at the airport, but he was eager to see her in person. Without bruises and swelling and scrapes, she'd likely be a knockout.

His phone rang and the readout showed his sister, Tyler.

[illegible] he responded, "Hi. How are you?"

"I'm good, Wyatt, how are you?" She sounded positive, which was a good sign.

He stepped from the room with a nod to Yvette and Jax and into the hallway, where he leaned against the wall.

"I'm fine. How's Dany?"

"Actually, that's why I'm calling. I wanted you to know that her graduation from high school was perfect and, of course, she graduated with honors. I think I mentioned it a while ago, but it came upon us so quickly with her birthday tomorrow and all. When I asked her if she wanted a party to celebrate, she just said dinner with her family and a few close friends would be perfect."

He inhaled deeply and held his breath until his lungs burned. Finally, exhaling he asked, "And does that include me?"

Tyler was quiet for a long time. So long in fact he wondered if the call had disconnected.

"Wyatt, she's coming around, I promise. But right now, she's noncommittal. Why don't you try giving her a call tomorrow, wish her a happy birthday, and see if you can get her to talk to you."

"Tyler, last time she barely said three words to me and hung up as soon as she could. I could tell she was struggling to be polite. But..."

"I know, Wyatt, but as she's matured, she's seeing things a bit differently. You simply need to show her you love her."

"I do love her, Tyler. But I don't know how to show her. I tell her, but she keeps saying, 'It's just words.'"

Tyler exhaled loudly, "I know. She barely knows you, so having you tell her you love her seems empty when you never see her."

He leaned his head against the wall and closed his eyes. "Maybe I can fly out there to see her. I can see where she lives and get to know her a bit better."

"You should ask her, Wyatt. Give her a call."

"I will, Tyler. In the meantime, do you need anything? I can send some money to help with the cost of the graduation dinner. Actually, I'll just do it whether you need it or not. I'll wire it."

"Wyatt, it isn't about money. You don't need to send any additional money this week. Your monthly support is more than enough. You're already paying for college. She says she's going to study to be a nurse."

He pushed himself off the wall with his shoulders, stood tall, and pulled his shoulders back holding them until the tension eased. "Tyler, it's how I show my appreciation for all you've done."

Her laugh on the other end of the line felt like a balm for his heart. It was genuine and instant.

"I do it because I love you. And I love, Dany. She's been a pleasure in my life. And since it turned out that I couldn't have my own children having Dany all these years has filled a hole I didn't know how I'd ever fill. Things work out, Wyatt. Trust in God to do that for us."

His phone buzzed that there was an internal message and though he didn't want to end his conversation, he didn't have much more to offer.

The clinic door opened and Jax and Yvette stepped into the hall a few feet from him.

"I love you, Tyler, thank you."

He ended his call and looked at the two women waiting for him to move forward.

Jax nodded, "Mrs. James buzzed. Dinner is ready in ten."

"Okay." He looked at Yvette. "Before we take your suitcase upstairs, do you have a laptop, iPad or any other electronic device that could have tracking software on it?"

Her eyes rounded and he saw the heavy swallow as her throat constricted.

"Ye...yes. My laptop."

Jax turned to Yvette. "Let Wyatt take your laptop. I'll show you my old room and then bring you down for dinner so you can meet those who are here."

Yvette leaned over her suitcase and unzipped an outer

compartment. Pulling her laptop from inside, she handed it to him, her face stiff. He assumed she was torn between embarrassment and fear.

"We'll take care of it and I'll bring it back to you as soon as Gaige locates any tracking devices on it and removes them."

Her face transformed to show her sadness; her eyes clouded. "I'm almost afraid to find out how much he actually knows about me. How could I not know that he was being so intrusive?"

Taking the laptop from her he tucked it to his side, "Because he's slippery and probably very practiced at this. You shouldn't feel any embarrassment over it. People like him are predators who make their living doing shit like this."

She simply nodded before Jax urged her on. "See you upstairs."

He walked the few steps to the conference room where the team computers and usually Gaige could be found. Opening the door, the lights in the room and the atmosphere of what they were all about surrounded him and the heaviness in his heart lifted. This is what kept him sane all these years. This and their work. Helping others, feeling needed. Being needed. Filling the gap.

Gaige, as usual, sat looking at a computer screen as words, letters, numbers, and a myriad of symbols scanned across the monitor.

"Yvette also has a laptop. Can you run your scan on this, too?"

Gaige turned in his seat and faced him. "Yeah, I'm scanning her phone now, I'll add this to the second computer and scan it while we eat."

He nodded as he set the laptop on the desk alongside Yvette's phone. "Thanks."

Gaige leaned forward, his green eyes probing his. "You okay?"

"Yeah."

"You seem kind of down and that's not like you. Is Dany okay? I'm here if you need to talk."

He nodded his understanding and turned to leave when Yvette's phone rang. He stopped to watch Gaige as he read the name on the screen and then turned it so Wyatt could see who was calling her. "John Caulfield."

"You going to answer it?"

[illegible] opulence of [illegible] organizing her thoughts.

"[illegible] God, Jax. I had no idea."

Jax laughed. "We work hard. Sometimes days at a time. But we make great money and when I lived here, we had everything we needed. It was designed with our needs in mind while at the same time camouflaging us from prying eyes so to speak. That's why Gaige chose a house and then added [illegible] underneath. We have the security of the underground lab and garage, which we can lockdown should someone be stupid enough to try to break in here. But other than anyone seeing us drive in or out, we don't have the cars all lined up for people to question what's going on at the compound."

Nodding and looking over the railing of the second floor down onto the large, opulent foyer below she could only say, "Wow."

Jax chuckled. "Dodge and I got married right down there in the foyer. Gaige and Sophie are getting married there in a week. You'll meet them at dinner. Fair warning,

Sophie will likely put you to work helping with some of the decorations. She's former military like me. But she's domestic unlike me. She isn't afraid to put anyone to work, so you'll notice the guys aren't hanging around a lot unless they're downstairs working out, shooting or just hiding in plain sight."

"She puts the guys to work. On decorations?"

This time Jax laughed. "Mostly building and moving things. She had them all building and painting benches last week for outside. There won't be a ton of people. We don't invite people who don't really know what we're all about. Except you now, but because I've known you forever and you needed help, I wasn't worried about you running off and telling folks. But Sophie wants seating outside after the ceremony because the weather is supposed to be nice. If it rains, well, we'll be inside."

Turning to look her friend in the eye, "Is that why you didn't have a huge wedding?"

This time Jax laughed from her belly. "You know I'm not a girly girl. And my mom had a fit through most of the planning because of it. Then she forbade me to wear my Army boots, so you must know I did. She wasn't happy with me, so when the day finally comes, Josh is going to have to deal with her wanting all the frills and a Catholic Mass, too. But having it here and wanting to keep it simple was the main reason we only had my mom, Dodge's parents and, of course, Josh. The only other folks were people associated with us. It was perfect actually."

Yvette reached forward and hugged Jax. Pulling away quickly she looked into Jax's eyes, "I'll get over feeling hurt I wasn't invited then. I felt left out. Now I don't."

Jax reached forward and took Yvette's left hand in both of hers. "I'm sorry you felt hurt and I should have explained it to you. We were on a mission when we set the date. When we got home, we literally threw the wedding together with other women's help and we kept it close."

Squeezing Jax's hands she smiled or tried to but with the swelling it undoubtedly didn't look like that at all.

Jax turned toward the right of the hall and walked toward the door across the hall but closest to the elevator that had brought them up here.

"This is your room now. I'll get you a key card to get in," Jax waved her card in front of the door and pulled the handle down. Following behind her friend an "ahh" escaped her throat at the beauty of the room. Earth tones and beautiful furniture greeted her.

"You can sit on the comfy sofa when you need a moment. The blanket on the bed is weighted, which I think you'll love. It's like being hugged all night long. It helped me a lot with my anxiety after Jake was killed."

Jax moved further into the room and to a door to the far right.

"This is your bathroom. If you need anything ask Mrs. James. She and her daughter, Kylie, clean and refill all supplies for us."

"Really? Oh my gosh, I've never had anyone clean for me." Tucking her hair behind her ear she noticed her hand shaking a bit and furrowed her brows as she looked down at her hand.

"It's the adrenaline leaving your body. We'll get you some food and then you can come up here and rest. In the morning you'll feel tons better."

Nodding at her friend, she walked to take a look at the bathroom. Jax turned and picked her suitcase up and lay it on the bed.

"Go ahead and wash up a bit. I'll wait out here and then take you down for dinner."

Stepping into the bathroom and closing the door she looked at herself in the mirror and her eyes welled with tears. Closing her eyes, she willed herself to pull it together, then she used the toilet, and washed her hands. As softly as she could she put cool water on her face. Using a washcloth laid out on her counter, she wet it, dabbed at her eye makeup now smudged and tried to straighten it up. Looking down at her clothing she opened the bathroom door and walked to her suitcase. Jax sat across the room on the sofa looking at her phone.

"I'm just going to throw some clean clothes on. I won't be long."

Jax looked up with a soft smile on her face. She could look soft and fuzzy sometimes and then she could look positively scary at other times. She was also the most unusual woman Yvette had ever known. Massively sure of herself while also being kind. At least to her.

"It's all good, Ette. When you're ready, we'll go down. I'm just sexting Dodge."

"Oh my god, TMI."

Unzipping her suitcase as Jax laughed, she pulled out a pair of jogging pants and a loose gauzy blouse hoping that the clothes wouldn't stick or abrade her wounds. Turning to the bathroom quickly she carefully pulled her clothes off and dressed. The soreness was still there, though her knees and elbows felt much better now.

Checking out the mess her hair was in, she finger combed it away from her face and deftly braided it down her head, pulling her long hair forward once it was diffi-cult to reach and continued braiding to the end. Holding the bottom of her braid between two fingers she walked from the bathroom to her suitcase, unzipped an inside pouch hoping she still had hair ties in there from her last trip because she sure didn't think to pack any.

Finding nothing she turned to Jax, "I don't suppose you have an extra hair tie on you?"

With a smile Jax stood and walked to the dresser on the left side of the room. Pulling the top drawer out, she opened a small plastic container and pulled out a dark tie. "Feel free to use these, I've still kept some things here in case we need to stay."

"Are you su..."

Jax held her hand up to stop her talking and smiling reached forward with the hair tie.

Taking the proffered tie, she quickly wrapped it around the end of her braid, flipped the braid over her shoulder and nodded.

"Okay, ready."

Her heartbeat increased at the thought of going down and meeting everyone at once, but the hospitality she was offered told her she needed to do this and be polite, especially since she needed to feel safe again.

"Okay, let's go see who's here."

14

———

...his eyes, still ...beers he'd had last ...with Axel and Gaige. The heaviness ...again settled in his heart. Today was Dany's birthday. She was eighteen years old and he barely knew her. He'd flipped out when his wife died in childbirth. He thought his life was over and what the fuck did he have to offer a baby? A girl at that. His sister, Tyler, was childless and desperate to have it. Having her take care of Dany while he finished his contract with the Army hopefully to get his head on straight seemed to be the balm for both of their wounds. Then he was recruited into GHOST 8 years later and he'd been here ever since. That was around 10 years now. Tyler was happy. Dany seemed happy and healthy and cared for. He'd tried now for the past 5 years or so to get closer to Dany so he could get to know her as her father. But she distrusted him and kept him at a distance. She'd really only known him these past years as a visitor. They'd never lived together as father and daughter and she called Tyler, Mom and Tyler's husband, Richard, Dad.

He fit visits in when he could, but his work took him places for days at a time. It was never regular hours and it was dangerous, so on some level he'd decided Dany was better off with Tyler and Rich and he'd touch base when he could.

Lifting his phone, the home screen popped on. 7:34 am. Breakfast would be served at 8:30. That gave him time to jump in the shower and see if Yvette would let him look at her wounds. And she'd likely be in need of Ibuprofen this morning.

Scraping his hands down his face he sat up, stretched, and gave himself a minute before making his way to the bathroom.

After showering, putting on his customary black t-shirt, black cargo pants and socks, he slipped into his boots. He grabbed his phone from the nightstand along with his wallet and his key card, which he kept on a badge reel on his waist. Opening the drawer of his nightstand, he pulled out his gun and holster, clipped them on, and headed toward the door. The aroma of bacon floated upstairs, and his stomach growled. Walking quietly to the elevator he swiped his card and tapped the down button. Within seconds the elevator appeared and the doors silently swished open.

"Can you hold the door?"

He turned to see Yvette limping slightly making her way to the elevator.

Reaching out to hold the door open for her, he watched her as she neared. The swelling had gone down quite a bit overnight. Her hair was hanging in long brunette waves. Fiery red hues shone where the overhead lights shined on her. Her eyes were clear today and she looked rested.

"Good morning. Did you sleep well?"

" God, I slept like a baby. How about you?"

He chuckled. "I slept good. A few beers will do that to you."

She smiled at him and nodded. Stepping into the elevator he noticed she wore jogging pants that hugged her ass perfectly. She had a sexy shape. Perfectly rounded cheeks that flowed both ways into a strong straight back and down shapely legs. Her feet were encased into slip on tennis shoes.

"How are you feeling? I was going to head down to the clinic and get fresh bandages and Ibuprofen for you this morning. Are you up for that before breakfast?"

"Thank you. Yes, I'm afraid I got my bandages wet this morning in the shower and took them off, but I don't want my clothing to rub against them all day."

Waving his card in front of the sensor he tapped the Conf. button and the elevator doors whooshed closed.

"I agree. It won't take long, and breakfast isn't for another few minutes, usually around 8:30. Breakfast is different than dinner. We just come when we're ready, but 8:30 is generally the time when everyone is here."

"Does Jax come each morning for breakfast?"

Glancing down at her, he saw her fingers lock together as if she were nervous.

"Sometimes. Sometimes Dodge cooks breakfast for them."

Yvette laughed. "She really isn't very domestic."

He laughed, too. "That is an understatement."

The elevator stopped and he waited for her to step off first, walking alongside her, he felt rather comfortable.

"Who's Dany?"

He stumbled slightly, caught himself and then kept going.

"She's my daughter. She just graduated high school."

"Okay." She continued walking, and he followed along. For some reason that knocked him off kilter a bit. Yvette stopped at the door of the clinic and turned to look up at him. "I heard you and Axel talking about her last night. Just some things like you don't know how to show her you love her, things like that. I wondered if she was a girlfriend or something."

He opened the door and stepped back for her to enter.

"No. No girlfriend here, I'm widowed. It's a hard life for a girlfriend. I never know when I'm leaving. I never know when I'll be home. Some women can't handle that."

"Sophie and the others do."

"Sophie and Gaige are different. Hawk and Roxanne are different. Megan and Skye are also..." He stopped for a minute and took in a deep breath. She smiled at him and his heartbeat increased.

"When you really love someone, you make it work. That's how you know she or he is THE one."

She turned and sat on the table and promptly began pulling up her pant leg. He prepared a tray with all the supplies he needed to rebandage her knees and elbows. He poured two Ibuprofen into a paper cup as he had yesterday, wheeled the tray to the table, and tended to her wounds while they chatted.

"You should call her. Dany. You show someone you love them by paying attention to them. Asking how they are and truly wanting the answer. Listen when she talks and ask her about it. How does she feel now that she's out of school? Things like that. Then call her again in a week. Ask about her again. Repeat."

He looked up into her gorgeous eyes, clear, bright, and earnest.

She reached out and lay her hand on his. "My parents died right after I graduated. I had to fend for myself most of the time. I cannot tell you how many times I wished I had a mom and dad to ask me how my day was and if there was anything they could do for me. "

The warmth of her hand seeped into his and he swallowed a large lump in his throat. He could feel the sting in his nose as emotions played over him.

Nodding, he moved his hand from under hers and began dressing her wounds. After breakfast, he'd call Dany.

they were sure. ...on his arms ran ...of his hands and she tried to study the shapes and forms to see if she could recognize anything in his tats. He looked up a couple of times and their eyes locked and the heat flushed up her chest and into her cheeks.

"Will you help me learn how to protect myself?"

It fell from her lips before she could think about it. He stopped applying ointment to her elbow and she heard him swallow.

"Sure. What did you have in mind?"

She shrugged. "I don't know. What should I know like karate or something?"

"I can show you Krav Maga. It's intense and I have to modify some moves for myself. I have problems with my knee if I'm not careful when I exercise. I do have exercises that help my knee. I have to keep it in shape for missions."

"I'm sorry. I'm totally fine with modified. It'll take me a

few days to heal enough that I don't hurt every time I bend my knees or elbows."

He handed her the Ibuprofen and a bottle of water and cleaned up the tray of discarded materials. A chime sounded and he pulled his gloves off to reach for his phone. His fingers deftly tapped and swiped, and she had a hard time looking away from them. He had nice fingers. He read a text, or something then said, "Jax won't be here today. She's exhausted from her mission and asked that I help you out. We could go over a few simple moves later this morning and just some basic self-defense that you can work on in your room to begin with."

"I'd like that."

"Jax also said your new phone is ready. We'll stop in the conference room to grab it on our way up to the dining room."

"Okay." She smiled and it didn't hurt today; she did feel a little pulling on the side of her face and there was some discoloration where her attacker punched her in the mouth yesterday. The bastard.

"Ready?"

"Yeah."

She scooted off the table and walked to the door where Wyatt waited. As soon as she approached, he opened the door for her, and they stepped out into the hallway. Striding next to her, he slowed as they approached a door on the right. He waved his key card in front of the sensor panel, then pushed the door open and waited for her to enter under his arm. Ducking under his arm was made easy given his height.

The room was bright and there was a wall of computers to the right and desks lined along the comput-ers. Gaige sat looking at several monitors. Gaige glanced over at them, nodded and then back to his computers. Without looking away from all the monitors in front of him, he reached into a drawer and pulled out a phone.

Wyatt stepped forward and took the phone from Gaige and pushed a button to turn it on.

"The basics?" He asked Gaige.

"Yeah. Our numbers, police, fire, etc. She can add her own numbers except Caulfield."

Her heartbeat ramped up and embarrassment surged through her as she assumed she was a nuisance. Then Gaige glanced around Wyatt once again, and Wyatt, as if just realizing he was standing between them, stepped to the side so she could see Gaige.

"Hi, Yvette. It's one of our phones, all of our team members' numbers are programmed in there. Feel free to add your family numbers if you need but not Caulfield. The software he had on your phone and your laptop would allow him to drop cookies with just a phone call. I'm cleaning some of that shit out of your phone and more out of your computer, but it will take a while as it's insidious and can hide itself in the most unsuspecting places. He has some quality stuff. But we may be able to use it."

She nodded. "He's a piece of work for sure and he does have money so he could buy the best. Thank you so much for all of your help."

Gaige laughed. "You shouldn't thank me yet. Sophie will be drafting you into wedding duty while you're here especially since Jax isn't coming in today."

She laughed right back. It felt good to be needed. This would help her feel useful and get to know the women better. "I'm happy to help out. Really. Otherwise I'd be sitting here doing nothing and worrying about everything."

Wyatt turned to her, "Do you have to call into your job? And will Caulfield try and cause trouble with your company?"

Tilting her head back to look up into his eyes, she swallowed. "I've been worrying about that a lot and he just might. I'll call the HR department and explain what's happened, sort of. I'm not going to tell anyone else anything, so they won't have any information to spill if John tries to contact some of my friends there. Not that anyone would, they all hated him. I don't know why I didn't see it all sooner. I feel like a moron."

Wyatt shook his head. "Don't be so hard on yourself. True psychopaths are very good at what they do."

Gaige opened a top drawer on the desk in front of him and pulled out a key card.

"This will get you into your room, the workout center and the elevator but not in here, or the shooting range. Sorry, that's for team members only, you'll need to be with one of us to access those rooms."

"Thank you again. I completely understand."

She turned to Wyatt. "You have a shooting range? Can you teach me to shoot?"

A laugh sounded behind her and Axel walked in.

"I'm a much better shot than Wyatt, you should be asking me to teach you."

Her cheeks fired red hot and she was at a loss. Luckily, Wyatt spoke up first. "Shut the fuck up. Twice. Twice in how many years you've out shot me. That does not make you an expert."

Axel laughed and walked further into the room. "That's right, you're the sharpshooter." Sitting at a desk on the other side of Gaige he said, "Breakfast is ready. I'm stuffed."

Wyatt turned and began walking to the door. "Are you hungry?"

"A bit."

"Let's go eat then we'll start training."

Exiting the room, she walked to the elevator and stopped in front of it.

"Try your key card and make sure it works."

She was actually excited to use it, which of course seemed rather silly, but it felt like a bit of trust. She waved her card in front of the sensor like she'd seen Wyatt do and she smiled when the doors opened with a whoosh.

Wyatt chuckled and walked in behind her.

They were quiet as the elevator lifted them to the main floor when she remembered. "Don't you have to call Dany today and wish her a happy birthday?"

[illegible] entered the [illegible] drinking a cup of [illegible] pointing at a list in front of her, raised her head up and smiled. Then she started talking.

"Yvette, Jax tells me you're fantastic at calligraphy. Would you please make place cards for the wedding tables?"

Yvette [illegible] bright [illegible] "I'd love to."

Sophie wrote on her list then looked up at him. Holding both hands up in front of him he shook his head. "Nope, Soph don't ask me to do anything. There are enough of women to do most of the list stuff. We guys are only going to move chairs, tables, and heavy things. The rest is up to you women."

"You women?" Sophie scoffed.

"You know what I mean. Plus, all the guys oddly arrived back from their missions last night. You've got a bunch to pick from."

She stared at him from across the table and he began to worry that she was about to chew him a new one. Her dark eyes bored into his amber ones and he knew he had to stand firm, or he'd be doing wedding shit all damned day. Staring back at her with a stone face she burst out laughing.

"You thought I was going to bitch you out."

"I did not."

Laughing louder she replied, "You so did. Jax has you guys scared shitless. I just love it here."

She dropped her head down and checked her list again.

Yvette giggled somewhat difficultly alongside him, and he looked down at her. Her eyes moved from Sophie to his. "You sure did look like you were scared."

"I did not." His voice rose an octave but then both women laughed again, and he chose to eat his breakfast and pray someone else would enter the room.

His prayers were answered five minutes later when Josh walked in. Setting a very full plate on the table at the far end, he sat and began digging in without a word to anyone of them.

Sophie cleared her throat, "Josh."

"No."

"No? No, what?"

"No, I'm not doing wedding junk. Call Jax. Or Megan. Or Skye. Roxanne's right upstairs."

He looked up finally and saw Yvette sitting at the table, pointed his empty fork in her direction and swallowed the food in his mouth.

"Have Yvette do something for you." As if he realized he hadn't said anything to her he continued. "Hi, Yvette. Long time no see."

Sophie glanced across the table at Yvette and winked at her.

"She's busy."

Josh's posture stiffened and his eyes landed on Yvette. Both women started laughing, which made Josh shake his head and shovel another bite of food into his mouth.

Lincoln and Skye walked into the dining room with filled plates and sat down. Skye sat next to Sophie and Lincoln to the right of Skye.

"Good morning," Skye addressed everyone. Looking across the table at Yvette her smile brightened.

"Hi, I'm Skye Winter and this is my husband, Lincoln."

Yvette smiled back at them. "I'm Yvette Jacobsen, Jax's friend."

"We don't live here. We just came over for the great breakfast."

"Do you live far from here?"

"No, our house is at the bottom of the Lynyrd Station on the Hill mountain, on the river. Jax and Dodge live on the opposite side of the river. Ford and Megan own the mountain except for what they sold to the guys before they were married. It's only about 15 minutes from here."

Josh spoke up at that moment. "Where are Jax and Dodge this morning? Dodge keeping her to himself?"

Wyatt looked down the table, once again feeling pride in his heart about this group of people he worked with and some he also lived with. He loved this part of his life. "She's tired," Wyatt said. "I spoke to her this morning."

Josh laughed then swallowed. "Jax is almost never tired."

"She is today."

Josh stopped chewing and looked up at him, his brows furrowed, then he looked over at Lincoln. Lincoln drank from his coffee cup then shrugged his right shoulder. "Dodge will be here in a bit, you can talk to him about it."

The briefest moment of silence followed then Josh took another bite of food. Conversation was the norm for them, bullshitting and small talk. Gaige appeared in the doorway and looked directly at him.

"Wyatt, we might have an issue. When you and Yvette are finished with breakfast come down to the conference room."

"Roger."

Glancing down at Yvette he watched her slowly set her fork on her plate, which still held half of her breakfast, then slowly drop her hands on her lap. As if sensing his gaze, her eyes met his and he saw the large swallow she took. He saw her heartbeat speed up by the pulsating in her neck. And the fear in her eyes made him angry. The possibilities were endless given Caulfield's money and connections. Based on pure speculation, Caulfield had made contact, had shit on her phone and computer implicating her or worst-case scenario he was in town and close. They could handle any issue even if the whole team wasn't home. But whatever it was, it meant Yvette was in danger.

Lowering his voice, he said, "Don't worry, we'll manage whatever is going on and I'll be here to help you all the way."

Her eyes filled with moisture, but she rapidly blinked it away, inhaled deeply, and then nodded her head.

Skye softly said, "Yvette. These guys, they've got mad skills. You're in the best of hands here. "And... looking down the table at Sophie, "we've been right where you are. It will all work out and you're safer at the compound than anywhere. Promise."

Yvette softly replied. "Thank you."

Sitting up straighter Yvette cleared her throat. "After we speak with Gaige, I'd love to hear your stories. That is if you want to tell them."

"What stories?"

Roxanne asked from the doorway as she and Hawk entered the room.

Sophie responded first. "Of how we came to be GHOST."

Roxanne's white-blond head bobbed up and down. "Oh, that could fill the rest of the day for sure."

Yvette smiled at Roxanne. "You, too?"

"'Fraid so." Roxanne sat on the other side of Yvette, Hawk on her other side.

Wyatt finished his breakfast and looked down at Yvette. "You going to finish your breakfast?"

"I don't want to be rude or offend Mrs. James, but my stomach is knotted up right now."

Sophie responded first. "She won't be offended and if you aren't hungry just take your plate back to the kitchen It's all good." Setting her pen down on her notebook Sophie finished. "When you're finished speaking with Gaige, come back up here and we'll chat about final wedding stuff and names for the place cards.

"I will."

Wyatt stood and waited for Yvette to stand. Grabbing his plate, empty cup, and silverware, he waited for Yvette to do the same and followed her into the kitchen. He heard some snickering behind him as he left the room, but he wasn't about to give them the satisfaction of turning and chatting about their crap. He wasn't interested in Yvette or her him. He felt sorry for her but, more importantly, responsible for her safety because Jax wasn't here. And he thought she was attractive. And appealing. And her sense of humor was beginning to show, he liked that. But that was it. Nothing more.

stomach news she Gaige's rigid posture was sign. She hoped above all hopes that she hadn't brought John here to cause trouble for these men and women who would place themselves in danger to protect her.

Gaige sat in his usual place in front of the computers

"I'll get right to the point. Caulfield is in town. I was able to pinpoint some of his software and send back tracking of my own to his phone. Turns out, he's here. So, he managed to use his tracking device on your phone, Yvette, before we got to your phone."

She wrapped her arms around her stomach in a protective move and took a couple of breaths before she spoke.

"Will he try to break in here? Should I leave so you all aren't dragged into my disaster? I could possibly get a flight to somewhere else."

Wyatt turned to face her. "No to all of that. You can't be out there on your own with that bastard tracking you."

"But now he won't be tracking me because Gaige took that stuff off my phone."

"Yvette, I didn't remove all of it just yet because I needed it to send tracking to his phone. Your phones are connected now so we can watch him. I figured he'd already tracked you here based on how quickly he was able to get in town."

Gaige leaned back in his chair. "I suspect he's already located this place, though he won't get in. I don't know what kind of manpower he has, but still, he won't get in. You're safer here than anywhere."

Gaige sat forward once again. "Wyatt is right. So, what we do is keep track of him. Though sending your phone on a flight somewhere could be a good diversion for a while. I'll think about that if we need time to put a plan in place."

She cocked her head to the side and watched his face. He seemed serious and then it dawned on her that that could be a good idea.

One of the computer monitors buzzed and Gaige and Wyatt both looked over at it. John's face came onto the screen from the outdoor camera she'd seen at the gates. She gasped loudly at seeing his face and wondered, not for the first time, what she ever saw in him.

Gaige looked over at her and said, "Don't say anything."

He waited for her to respond but all she could do was nod.

He tapped a key on his computer. "How can I help you?"

"I'd like to speak to Yvette."

"There's no one here by that name," Gaige responded.

She saw John's jaw clench; he had a fuse about as long as a gnat's hind leg.

"I happen to know she's here."

"Sorry, dude, no she isn't. Only people here are my family."

"Look, asshole, I'm not in the mood to be fucked with. Send Yvette out here or I swear to God, I'll bust in and take her."

"That would be the biggest mistake you ever made. Guaranteed." His lowered voice revealed a deadly calm certain to instill fear.

Wyatt's posture next to her stiffened, his hands fisted, and he looked ready to reach into the camera and pull John through it.

"We'll see whose mistake it is, asshole."

John threw his car into reverse and slammed his foot on the gas. His brakes squealed as he shifted into drive and took off.

Gaige turned the camera to watch him drive away, tapped a couple of times, and then pulled up the pictures of the car John was driving and the license plates on a computer screen.

"I'll run these," he said before turning back to them.

Wyatt spoke first. "We keep her here and make sure she isn't seen. You'll keep tracking Caulfield and we'll know if he's still close. What happens next is his move, which I suspect is to try to get into the compound."

"I think you're correct on that. I'll call everyone down and put the whole team and staff on alert. We need to be hyper-vigilant coming and going that he doesn't try to squeeze through the gates on foot. Not sure how bold he is, but let's not take any chances."

She finally found her voice. "He'll be very bold. He knows that I've seen his laptop and know about his sex trafficking operation and the deposits into his bank accounts. He's worried that I'll talk to the authorities."

"In a sense you have, Yvette. I haven't said anything to my contact at the State Department, but we can get information to the proper authorities and take his operation down in good time. But we need to do it in a way that he doesn't learn that it came from you. We also need to gather more information to try to locate those women you spoke to and any other women that can be traced to him. It's likely they are still alive otherwise there's no profit in it for him. If he's involved in sex trafficking, he may want a large group of women to move out at once," Gaige said, "depending if he's selling them in the United States or internationally. If he's selling them to select buyers in this country, they may be harder to find. Whatever he's up to, we'll bring him and his operation down."

Her nerves began to fray even further. "No, I'm complicit. He made me help him; though I didn't know what I was doing. And I feel responsible and I need to help those women. I duped them into going with his men, or at least kept them there long enough for their guard to be down. It's my fault."

"If you didn't know what you were doing, you aren't guilty," Gaige responded.

Wyatt placed his hand on her shoulder. "Gaige is right. It doesn't really work that way. And if authorities can find the women you spoke to, they'll confirm you were only chatting with them in a bar. John duped you into helping him, and he made a great profit using you. He might have had a passing thought that you'd figure it out. He probably was convinced that if you did find out it would be accidentally, and he could control you by telling you that you were an accomplice to make you stay quiet. I don't think he thought you had the guts to hack into his email account. Once he found out you had, he said he'd kill you."

Her knees shook, and for a moment she felt like she was about to lose her breakfast. Turning the chair next to Gaige, she sat down and tried to breathe deeply to get her emotions in check. Now was not the time to panic. What would Jax do at a time like this?

"Unless they're mad at me and want me to suffer."

She turned to Wyatt, "I guess now is a good time to start training me to defend myself."

He nodded. "Right after Gaige finishes briefing everyone. Hang tight, they'll be here in a few minutes."

She looked over and Gaige had just finished sending a group message to the team she suspected. Before that thought left her mind, Axel walked in, sweating profusely, as if he had been working out. Soon other members began entering the room and circling the table. She was introduced to the final couple of people, Dodge and Ford with the exception of Ford's wife, Megan, she hadn't met last night or this morning. She saw instantly upon looking around the room that it was filled with brawn, brains, and men and Sophie, ready to fight and protect. It was stunning, this room of people and she finally saw the full force backing her. Only missing was Jax to complete the group. She was honored and humbled to be here amongst these people. Hopefully. she wouldn't get any of them hurt or, worse, killed, while they, and whoever they may need at the State Department, took John down. That thought made her stomach quell once again.

Gaige stood and walked to the conference room table. "We've got a bit of a situation here."

...couldn't ... Maybe today he'd ... and taken it up. He could use a ... well. Taking the phone from his back pocket he scrolled for his barber's phone number and tapped the call icon.

Walking around the room to gather his belongings including his gun, wallet, key card. He made an appointment for a haircut before working. Exiting his room, he walked down the stairs to help loosen his knee and stretch before working out. He'd go easy on Yvette; she still had injuries and wasn't used to this type of workout.

In the foyer area below he found Sophie, Megan, Roxanne, and Skye talking about wedding plans and who was to do what. When they looked over at him at the bottom of the steps, he held both hands up in front of him.

"Just going down to exercise."

A couple of the women laughed at him, then turned to finish their discussion.

Yvette began descending the stairs behind him and he turned at the sound of her steps. Besides the bandages on her knees, his first thought was "Holy shit". About 5'6" inches of lean body, she had creamy white skin encased in tight fitting workout shorts and a tank top. Her brown hair was piled high on her head, her eyes, those tawny orbs, focused on his. Knockout was not a good enough word to describe the beauty before him.

"Yvette, when you're finished with your training, we'll be in the dining room," Sophie called.

Yvette turned her head to look over the railing; the smile she gave to those women was stunning.'

"I'll be there shortly."

She turned her head back to him, her smile still in place, "Ready to show me how to kick ass?"

He snorted because he didn't expect it. "Yep, let's go."

He walked next to her to the elevators reminding himself that he wasn't interested in her for anything other than protecting her. Also, he just wanted to make sure she could protect herself. Nothing more. Not really.

As they stepped off the elevator at the lower level he said, "So we need a code word to use. Something to say if you get in trouble, and you're with people and don't want them to know that you are calling for help. So, a common word or phrase that won't raise anyone's suspicions. For instance, "I'm still shopping." Or "I'd like to stay for a few hours.""

"Okay. How about that one? 'I'd like to stay for a few hours '. It seems logical but no one says that very often. Normally you'd say a few days, a bit longer, things like that."

He nodded. "Great, that's your code phrase."

Watching her response, she merely nodded as if that were finished and now on to the next item of business.

He opened the exercise room door and held it for her. Briefly glimpsing at her perfectly shaped ass as she passed him, he admired the view, then followed her inside. He wasn't interested in that. Her. A relationship.

"So first we stretch. Sit on the mat and follow what I do. Only do it to your level of comfort so you don't pull a muscle or hurt yourself. And, for the time being, until your wounds have healed a bit more, you don't want to break them open again. So, when you feel pulling on them don't keep going."

"Okay." She sat across from him and he straightened his legs out in front of him and leaned over them grabbing his toes and pulling himself lower over his legs. He counted to 20 in his head sat up, then stretched again.

"Did you call Dany?"

The air whooshed from his lungs and he sat up. Their eyes met and a slow smile spread across her face.

"What? I just wondered and I'm trying to make conversation."

He inhaled deeply, held his breath a few seconds, and then slowly let it out.

"No."

"Why?" She put her hands behind her on the mat and leaned back. "You're scared."

"I am not."

He leaned over again so his eyes didn't give away his little fib. He was scared. For some stupid reason it seemed as if he made this call count and Dany didn't agree to see him that she'd slip right out of his life forever. It might be stupid, but she was growing up and getting ready to embark on her own life.

She scooted closer to him. "Would it help if I were here coaching you along? You know, kind of like Cyrano, but of course not the romantic part."

"It might."

"You're helping me and this way at least I'll feel like I'm paying you back."

He groaned. This wasn't at all how he thought this day was going to go. Then again, he didn't expect yesterday to go like it did either.

"Come on, let's call her now and you'll feel better. I promise. But most importantly, Dany will feel better, too."

Well, that might be true, he did want Dany to feel better about him as a person. Then, maybe as a dad. Or at least, as the man who fathered her and loved her. They shared blood. Family. According to Tyler, they shared mannerisms, the same sense of humor, and a few other characteristics, too. He'd seen it in the pictures and videos Tyler had sent him.

Inhaling again, he pulled his phone from the back pocket of his shorts and tapped to find her number. His stomach convulsed. He always got nervous talking to Dany.

"Maybe we should do this later."

Yvette lay her hand on his bare knee and the warmth in her touch made his heartbeat increase.

"Let's call her now."

Staring into her eyes, he saw her earnest desire to help him.

He tapped Dany's picture, then the speaker on his phone so Yvette could hear Dany, too.

"Hello?"

"Hi, Dany, it's da...Wyatt."

"Hi."

A few seconds went by and Yvette nudged him and mouthed. "Happy Birthday."

"Happy Birthday, Dany. I hope you have a great day planned."

"Thanks." Her voice sounded less than enthusiastic, but more positive than the last time he spoke to her "

"So far my plans all seem to be falling apart. I was planning a trip for the coming week with friends and they all had to cancel for one reason or another. I so wanted to have an adventure; you know, do something different before I start college. I'm majoring in nursing."

Yvette nudged him and mouthed. "Have her come here."

He shook his head and said, "I'm sorry. Maybe your plans will still come together."

"No, they won't. It's just too busy for everyone right now and then we'll all be off to college. We'll be all over the country. But before that I had hoped to have an adventure doing something unusual."

Yvette nudged him again, but he couldn't get the words out and shook his head no.

Then, she just blurted out, "Come here."

His mouth fell open as he stared at her in disbelief.

"Who is that?"

"Hi, Dany, I'm Yvette. I'm a friend of your dad. Well, actually Jax, but she's still sleeping, and your dad is helping me learn how to defend myself. Come here and let him teach both of us self-defense. We'll have fun together and I won't feel stupid being the only newbie. I don't know anyone else here either, except Jax, who is super busy, and we're having a fun wedding in a week."

Dany's laugh on the other end of the phone was a pleasant sound. Not to be completely upstaged he added,

"That sounds like a great plan, Dany. You can stay in Yvette's room with her and I can show you around the place and a little of what I do. I can teach you self-defense and we can get to know each other better. Then we can go to Gaige and Sophie's wedding and celebrate with my teammates. That's something unusual and adventurous."

Yvette's smile was gorgeous. It lit up the room and his heart nearly burst when Dany replied, "I can be there tomorrow."

going to be fun. [...] to keep her mind off [...] terrifying situation if that were [...] And she was helping Wyatt mend his relationship with his daughter. What could be better?

"What in the world did you do that for?"

His tone was distant, his eyes were unfriendly, and he took on a frustrated aura.

"I'm helping you and Dany get to know each other."

He groaned. "I don't think you understand, Yvette. I haven't spent more than an hour or two alone with Dany since she was born. I know that sounds bad, but when she was first born, my wife died. In childbirth. I couldn't deal and my sister stepped in to raise her. When I came home on leave, I'd visit, but she didn't know who I was. Then about eight years ago when I tried to really get to know her, she started asking questions. And then she got mad because I hadn't been around. I'd stayed in the service rather than raise her. I'd lost my wife and I was grieving. What did I know about babies? At the time it seemed like

Tyler was the answer for both of us. I suppose I could have moved in with Tyler, but I didn't think that would be fair to Tyler. She and Richard deserved a life on their own. Now, you've got her coming here for an extended period and... Well, what the fuck am I supposed to do with her?"

Her back tensed and her brows furrowed.

"What does that mean? She's not a little baby anymore, she's a grown woman. You don't have to DO anything with her. You said you wanted to spend time with her and get to know her so do that. Take her shopping. Show her the town. Show her a bit of what you do. Ask her questions about her. Learn her favorite color. Her favorite television show. Her favorite ice cream. How is this all so foreign to you?"

She saw him swallow and his shoulders hunched forward a bit. Those big, strong, massive shoulders slumped in defeat. It tugged at her heart.

"Oh." It dawned on her then. "You've simply retreated from relationships?"

The only recognition that he'd heard her was the slight lift and fall of his shoulders.

"Oh, Wyatt. I am so sorry." She leaned over and wrapped her arms around his shoulders and laid her head on his left shoulder. "I had no idea."

They sat that way for a while. It was nice. Comforting in a way even though he didn't hug her back. She felt the tension leave his body small increments at a time. "But you've managed to make relationships with your coworkers. So, you know how to do it."

He remained quiet. Then she softly said, "I'll help you with her. I'll be here. You can show us how to defend ourselves and when you need a break, you just need to give me a code word and Dany and I will go and do something for a while."

"Way to spin that back to me."

She giggled into his shoulder and color her surprised when she liked the way she felt against him. He smelled good. The sides of his beard tickled her nose, but she could also feel the softness in those little hairs. The thought of running her fingers through his beard sent a tingle down her spine

"Did you grow the beard to hide your scar?"

"Nah, I've gotten used to people staring at it. It was just time for a change."

"I only see your dimples. And your eyes, they are the most unusual color."

He softly responded, "Says the woman with the tawny eyes."

Sitting up abruptly, she pulled back and resumed her former position across from him.

"I guess we'd better get this first session in so I can go and write out some place cards for Sophie and see what else she has for us to do. Tomorrow we'll be busy with Dany."

His phone pinged and he looked down at it.

Clearing his throat, "Dany just sent her flight itinerary and what time to pick her up at the airport tomorrow. That girl moves quick."

Yvette giggled. "She really did want to get away for a while. I think it's cute."

His brows raised and his eyes closed as if fighting off exasperation.

"I hope this isn't a mistake."

"It won't be. We'll have fun together."

His sigh was aggravated. "Okay, let's finish up here, I've got a haircut appointment in about an hour.

She looked at his hair. It was dark and long to cover the scar. A lump rose in her throat at the thought of some woman, probably scantily clad, running her fingers through his hair and him enjoying it. But that was stupid. They were barely friends.

"Just a trim, I hope. You've got great hair.

"I don't know about that, but yeah just a trim."

There was a silence for a moment, so he said, "Okay, back to stretching."

His voice brought her around to the task at hand and she leaned over her legs as far as she could and held to lengthen her muscles. Once they'd done this a couple of times, he broke into her thoughts again.

"Okay, today I'll show you one move. You can practice it on your own and tomorrow show me how you've done."

"Okay."

"So, the first thing you need to know and take in is it's as much in your mind as your body. We'll start with the Neutral Stance, which is the first move, so to speak. So, legs shoulder width apart, arms down, footing not perfect. Look as neutral as you can. Your attacker should not be aware that you are preparing for battle. But in your mind, you are getting ready for battle. That's very important."

He demonstrated a neutral position and she mimicked his stance. He smiled and walked around her, she assumed to assess her stance. He jabbed at her shoulder from behind and her body moved forward. She looked back at him, her brows furrowed, and he laughed.

"You weren't ready for battle with that namby-pamby stance."

"You said to look neutral."

"Right, but I also said you should be ready for battle. You weren't."

He walked in front of her and assumed his stance once again.

Looking her in the eye he said, "Do I look ready for battle?"

"No."

"Try to push me."

Stepping forward two steps, she shoved his shoulder. He didn't budge, not an inch.

Her brows furrowed again, and she tried pushing him once more. This time he surprised her and wrapped his arms around her and held her tightly to his body. She squirmed and wriggled trying to get free, but he held firm.

His voice was low when he spoke, his breath warm against the side of her face, the bristles on his face lightly brushed her cheek.

"You weren't ready again."

She stopped squirming and froze. Mostly because his strength was impressive. His body felt amazing against hers. His voice low and growly shot emotions and sensations through her entire body. Her reaction moved her more than she wanted to admit.

His strong arms released her, and she stepped back. The instant flush of blood rushed up her chest, neck and cheeks and she was slightly embarrassed that he'd seen he affected her in such a way.

"Assume the neutral stance again. Be ready for battle but look as if you aren't."

Shaking her head once and closing her eyes, she silently chastised herself for getting flushed and all girly. She needed to learn this stuff and keep her head on straight. Feet shoulder width apart, not evenly spaced but her right foot slightly back. Raising her head and tossing her ponytail back from her shoulder, she leveled a gaze on him and silently dared him to try that again.

A slow, sexy, lethal smile moved across his handsome face and butterflies came alive in her stomach. Slowly he walked around, his eyes assessing, his movements deliberate. She didn't know where or when he'd try to catch her off-guard, she just assumed it would happen. Her heartbeat increased the longer it took him to test her. From behind her he leaned in and whispered close to her ear.

"You look sexy as hell."

She turned her head in his direction and in an instant his arms came around her from behind and her body was once again pressed against his, trapped in an iron grip he slightly lifted her off the ground as she struggled again to free herself. Then she felt him grow rigid, the unmistakable thickness of his penis pushing against her ass and her body reacted like a volcano about to erupt.

hammered, [...] into something alto- [...] than he had intended. Slowly releasing Yvette, his voice was gruff when he finally managed to say, "Practice your neutral stance. I have to get ready for my haircut."

He stalked from the room without giving her a backwards glance. He hurried to the elevator and tried to think of [...] anything he'd need to force his erection down as quickly as possible. Afraid to look down at himself to see if it was noticeable, he stared straight ahead, but then the fragrance of fresh soap mixed with a slight muskiness reached his nostrils and they flared. The elevator doors opened, and he glanced down at Yvette at the same time she looked up at him. Her cheeks were flushed, and her nipples protruded through the tight top she wore. Despite the bruising on the side of her face, those mesmerizing eyes were about the most beautiful ones he'd seen in years.

She stepped in the elevator just ahead of him. His

crotch was pulsing, his body was taught and every sense he had was on high frequency.

As the door slid shut, he turned to face them, but stopped when he faced Yvette and saw her tongue slip from her lips and swirl around slightly, wetting them. The overhead lights caught the slight sheen and his blood pulsated through his body almost painfully. As if there were a magnet between them he stepped one step toward her at the same time she stepped toward him and he lost the battle of wills he was having with himself.

His head bent and his lips were on hers in an instant. He felt her hands grab both sides of his shirt and hang on and his hands reached around her and pulled her tightly to him so she could feel his hard-thrumming erection pushing against her body.

He heard her whimper and her fists tightened in his shirt.

Her lips were soft against his. Her tongue delved into his mouth and his tongue warred with hers in such a frenzy he almost felt as though she'd consume him. His head tilted slightly so his mouth fit against hers perfectly and she whimpered again. A grunt sounded in the small space his brain barely recognizing that it had come from him. Her body so tight against his and her breasts pushed into his chest magnifying her softness felt amazing against him. His fingers itched to feel more of her, and he dropped his hands and squeezed her delicious ass as he pulled her into his aching cock, which earned him another whimper.

Cool air surrounded him as well as the tsk of a female voice. He pulled away as his brain came back to earth from wherever it had flown. He turned to the elevator doors to see Jax, her left shoulder leaning against an elevator door, her arms crossed over her chest, her eyes locked on his, and her jaw clenched tightly.

"Jax, we were just..."

"I saw what you were doing. Of course, you both can sleep with whomever you want, your adults. But I'm giving both of you this warning, and I mean it."

Her eyes darted to Yvette's and he was grateful she hadn't looked down to see his erection, which was now beginning to soften.

"I work with Wyatt. I have for a number of years. If things get hot and sweaty with you two and then you leave him brokenhearted, I still have to work with him."

"I know. I'm sorry, it just happened."

Jax didn't wait. Her eyes landed on his.

"Yvette is about the only friend I have left from high school. I don't stay in touch with anyone else. Just her. If things get rolling between you and don't work out, she will still be my friend and I don't want any bullshit from you. Plus, I'll be pissed at both of you."

He cleared his throat but Jax continued.

"You two do what you want. I just don't want to have to pick up the pieces of either of you. Am I understood?"

Yvette responded first. "Yes, you are understood."

He found his voice then. "Understood." Then he had a surge of anger run through him and he finished with, "But understand this Mrs. Sager. If Yvette and I want to be together no matter the length of time, you need to stay out of it. You've had your say."

Jax stared at him for a long time. He'd always thought she was a beautiful woman. Something about her today almost sparkled. Her dark hair shined against the lights, her dark eyes were clear and sharp and didn't miss much. She was impressive that way. Her full lips had a hint of shine on them, something that was new since she and Dodge had gotten together. Then those lips turned up into a smile.

"I have and so have you." She then looked at Yvette. "You have a few minutes to talk to me or are you two on your way upstairs to have at it?"

Yvette smiled at her friend and it was beautiful. "Wyatt has a haircut appointment so we can talk."

Jax smirked at him, took a step back to allow him to step off the elevator, then giggled slightly as he walked the few steps down the hall to his rooms.

He refused to look back at them but was grateful his boner had softened so he didn't walk funny. Waving his card in front of his door he stepped inside looking straight ahead. As soon as his door closed he was sorry he hadn't leaned down and kissed Yvette's lips once before walking away. It would have shown Jax and Yvette that he...he what? Was serious? He wasn't fucking serious. He was...

Fuck, he didn't know what he was. Wait, he was horny. He thought Yvette was stunning. Her body felt fantastic against his. He didn't remember a time when a woman pressed against him felt like that. Horny – that was it.

... the women ... continued ... wedding guest list. It wasn't a long list, but Sophie wanted things to be nice, not overly formal but elegant in a simple way.

"Emersyn's name is spelled differently but it's so pretty in writing," she said out loud to no one in particular. The other women were either talking or working on bows or floral ...

Sophie looked up from the purple ribbon she was cutting and smiled. "That's Gaige's niece. His sister, Keirnan, is married to Dane. Their other two children are Hayden and Elise."

Skye looked up from the purple bow she was making. "Is Emmy still in the Army?"

"Yep, she was able to get leave to be here for the wedding. So are Hayden and Elise. It's almost a miracle that they all were able to snag leave at the same time. I'll bet Dane and Keirnan are super excited to be with all of them at one time again."

Roxanne continued arranging the Lavender, Lisianto, Lilacs and baby's breath in little glass jars to be set on each table. The flowers were all artificial but looked so real she wanted to lean down and sniff them.

"I can only imagine," Roxanne was gorgeous and so ethereal. She gave off a cool vibe; perhaps it was her lawyer MO. When Yvette had first seen Roxanne and Hawk together, her initial thought was they were stunning. He was massive, dark, and broody. She was tall, thin, and her wavy, silver-white hair shone brightly under any light. He liked touching her. He was always holding her hand or pressing his hand at her lower back.

"My family wasn't together very often after we all went our own directions. My brothers found it hard to get leave and when they were deployed, it was out of the question." Roxanne finished.

Wyatt appeared in the doorway; his large frame blocking the kitchen behind him. Yvette looked up at him and smiled when his eyes sought out hers. He was freshly showered, and the aroma filtered into the warm room and gave her goose bumps. He smelled manly, clean, and spicy like cloves. Yum.

He nodded. "Everything okay here?"

"Yep." She held up a place card she'd just written out with Emersyn's name and his brows rose then fell.

"I'm off to get my hair cut. You should make out a place card for Dany, too. Sophie, she'll be here for the wedding, hope you don't mind."

Sophie looked up and smiled at him. "Really? That's awesome, Wyatt. She's more than welcome of course."

He grinned. It was cute. Not cute, handsome, and maybe a bit shy. His eyes landed on hers again. "See you later."

"Okay." Her cheeks flamed bright red as he turned and left the room and all she could think was that she wanted to run after him and kiss him goodbye. But she didn't know if he wanted that. She sure did. But then she scolded herself for her behavior earlier. She'd really only known him a day, well, two now, and here she was throwing herself at him like a slut. Just because he was nice to her and was helping to train her didn't mean he really liked her. Most unattached men would sleep with a woman if she threw herself at them. She knew she was attractive enough and didn't have self-esteem issues in that area. It made her second guess herself as to why in the hell she stayed with John when she knew what slime he was. She had no business making relationship decisions, clearly, she wasn't that good at it.

"Well now, look at that. Wyatt seems to have a stronger interest than training you in self-defense." Jax's voice held some humor and a couple of the other women giggled.

"He was just being nice," Yvette responded, but the fire in her cheeks belied her thrill at Jax's words.

Jax leaned forward and looked her in the eye. Her focus solely on Yvette now. "I think it might be more than that."

She swallowed as she looked into Jax's eyes. Deciding a subject change was needed she responded. "You really do look tired, Jax. Are you alright?"

Jax's nose wrinkled but she sat back in her chair, swiped her right hand through her long glossy hair and said, "Yeah. I guess I've let myself get run down lately. We're going to take a few days off this week and chill. Right now, there aren't any missions running, so it's a good time to wind down and regroup."

Megan got up and walked around the table to Jax's

side and instantly lay her hand against Jax's forehead. The nurse in her always came through.

"You don't feel feverish, so that's good. When was your last physical? You should probably go in and make sure your blood pressure is good and that you aren't anemic and that everything is working as it should be."

Jax tilted her head back and looked up at Megan. "I'm fine. I will if I still feel tired tomorrow."

Megan patted Jax's shoulder and resumed her previously vacated seat.

Gaige walked into the dining room and went immediately to Sophie. Leaning down he kissed her temple and did a quick glance at the table and all the flowers, ribbons, wires, tape, place cards and miscellaneous items strewn across it. Giving his head a quick shake, he then looked directly at Yvette.

"Yvette, are you willing to talk to our contact at the State Department about Caulfield's activities? He's asking to speak with you, and we can do it in the conference room downstairs via conferencing software."

She sat up straight, lay her pen down, and looked at Gaige. "Yes. I'll tell them everything they need to know. Or ..." She shook her head. "Everything I know. They'll likely need more information than what I have, but I'll help out in any way I can."

He nodded. "Great. I have a call scheduled with him in an hour. Text me and I'll let you into the conference room."

Jax sat forward. "I'll bring her down, then I'll step out and go home. I need a nap."

Gaige looked across the table at Jax and studied her for a moment. As she was learning was his style, he simply nodded, then left the room.

Her stomach summersaulted at that moment as things were being set in motion. She wanted to bring John down. The crap he was dealing in presumably the kidnapping and sex trafficking had to stop. It would likely put her in grave danger though. It already had. But telling all she knew about John would effectively put a target on her back. No matter how hard anyone tried to keep her out of it, John would certainly know it was she who turned on him. Wasn't that why he'd followed her here? To stop her. The real question now was just how far he would go. She forced herself to remember that she had a covert operation the government used, namely, GHOST, on her side.

Dany's stomach twisted. He wanted to develop a relationship with Dany, and this felt like the first step, but what if he couldn't do it? He'd probably never get another chance. He felt like he was tiptoeing on quicksand so, he'd sink fast. He'd never been a father. It had been his decision and he could admit it though it was painful. Susanna, his deceased wife, would have been deeply disappointed in him, to see how he had allowed things to turn out between him and Dany. But, after she died, he just couldn't do it.

The first passengers began to walk into the terminal from the plane and his stomach summersaulted violently. Afraid again he'd lose its contents, he took a deep breath. He popped a mint into his mouth, which had always worked to quell his nausea, and hoped for the best. It was all he could do at this point. And, if Susanna was watching over him, like he'd often felt over the years, she'd help him and Dany develop a father-daughter relationship now.

Passenger after passenger walked through the door and he was brought back to a few days ago when Yvette had walked through the door battered and bruised. He had to fight the surge of anger that flared just at the thought of it. Then fear erupted as he thought of Dany in the same circumstance. He'd kill anyone who tried to hurt his girl. They may not have had a close relationship all these years, but she was still his daughter. His blood. His family.

A beautiful dark-haired young woman walked through the door and he marveled at the fact that she was stunningly like Susanna but there was much of him there, too. Black hair, amber-colored eyes – that was him. But she was tiny, only around 5' tall, her short spunky hair style framed her petite face perfectly – that was Susanna. Pride flooded through him at the lovely creature, his daughter, before him. Stepping toward her, he stopped hesitating as to what to do now. Did she want him to hug her? Should he or was that too forward? Faced with indecision he tried swallowing the lump in his throat, but it went down with great difficulty. Then, she looked right at him and his heart hammered in his chest. This moment they'd both remember for the rest of their lives, hopefully in a good way, stretched into what felt like minutes.

Her lips trembled and he saw her swallow and realized she was young, likely unsure of herself, and probably just as nervous as he was. Moving toward her he smiled, which probably didn't look all that welcoming since it felt forced to him, "Hey, Dany. It's great to see you again."

She smiled and stepped forward with her arms out and relief flooded through him when she wrapped her arms around his waist. Hugging her close it struck him how tiny she was compared to him.

"It's great to see you, too. Where's Yvette?"

He stood back fighting the disappointment that she was eager to see Yvette and not just him.

"She's at the compound."

"Compound? You live in a compound?"

He rubbed the back of his neck with his right hand. "It's what we call it."

She looked into his eyes and he felt another burst of pride at the intelligence in them and sheepishness at whether he met her standards as a father. Her eyes roamed down his heavily tattooed arms and hands then back up to his face, landing on the scar on the side of his face and neck, that she knew was there but camouflaged by his beard.

"How did you get that?"

His left hand went immediately to the left side of his face and neck and lower over the scar and under his hair.

"I got this on a mission in the rain forest five years ago in a fight with a high knife-wielding suspect. Axel subdued the suspect saving my life. Axel has one, too, as a result but on his right cheek."

"I can't wait to see Axel with the matching scar. Who else will I meet at this compound?"

He looked around for a suitcase, saw none, then held his hand out for her to walk with him to the baggage area, continuing their conversation as they walked.

"There are a number of us who live there, and you'll meet them all. Maybe it's better to meet them one at a time."

She shrugged. "Okay, tell me about Yvette, your 'friend '". She let go of his hand to finger quote.

Instantly remembering how Yvette felt pressed against

him his cheeks flushed crimson, the heat suddenly causing him to sweat.

"She's a friend of Jax's who needed help. I'm training her in self-defense techniques. She's been abused by a former boyfriend and she's hiding out at the compound while we bring the jackass down."

Glancing down at Dany his heart beat faster when her eyes met his.

"Holy cow. Poor Yvette."

"Yeah. The rest of the story is for her to tell you, not me."

She shrugged again and they continued walking.

"Tell me about you, Dany. You said you'll be off to college to study nursing. Where are you going to school? "

"Well, I'm planning to go to Boston College in the fall. It's something I've always wanted to do. Mom tells me that's what my mother did for a living before she died."

That startled him. Mom. He knew she called her aunt her mom. He'd set that into motion. It made sense of course, Tyler was the only mom she'd ever known. It just hurt to hear it.

"Wyatt? Did you hear me?"

Wyatt, she called him Wyatt. Not dad. He knew she called Tyler's husband, Richard, dad. That hurt more.

Clearing his throat, he took in a deep breath, pushing those negative feelings down. Way down. Then responded to her. "Yes, your mom was a fantastic nurse. She was the best. She was beautiful. Everyone loved her."

"Is that how you met? You're a medic, right?"

"Yes, it's how we met. Susanna, your mom, was also in the Army and was stationed at the same base I was. We met, fell in love and married."

"That's cool." They walked along in silence for a time,

navigating the throngs of people, the various corridors and reading the signs.

Finally coming into the baggage claim area Dany saw the baggage carousel her luggage was to be on and pointed to it, but it wasn't rotating yet, so they stood together quietly. Within a few minutes, a loud horn sounded, and the carousel began to move.

Looking down at her he said, "Tell me when you see your suitcase and I'll go get it for you."

"Okay." She twisted the gold stud earring in her right ear then said, "On the way home can we talk about your decision to let Mom and Dad raise me?"

"Yes, we can talk about that."

[illegible] panel of the [illegible] leaned forward and [illegible] she looked at Jax and her friend [illegible]

"I'm heading home. I won't be back for supper, but I think you're in good hands here."

The smile that Jax gave her was sly, sweet, and teasing.

"I'll manage. Thank you for letting me use your room while I'm here."

"I really only use it now when we've come back from a long mission and are waiting for everyone to arrive for a debrief and we're exhausted. I'm glad it's available for you to use."

"You seem happy, Jax. Dodge seems like a great guy. I never thought I'd see the day you would be married; you've always been so independent."

Jax laughed. "Yeah, he's the one for sure. Like everyone, I think, we work on our relationship. He doesn't place a ton of demands on me, he understands I love what I do, and he shares that love of the job. Of course, all the sexy times are amazing. I love talking to him about almost everything. I'm making it sound as if it's all about what Dodge has to do or be for me. It's not. He's easygoing, but I don't push it. Believe it or not, I rein in my temper a lot and sometimes I even apologize because I know how lucky I am. Sometimes he thinks I take too many chances, but I think he does. We argue, we laugh, we compete. It's good. Plus, he can cook. Do NOT tell Megan or Skye that he can cook. He had them convinced before we were married that he couldn't cook so they were always dropping off meals for him. Well, they know I can't cook, so they've kept dropping things off!"

"Gosh, that's fantastic, Jax. I won't say a word to Skye or Megan." Jax's smile said it all, then Yvette remembered Dany. "Tonight, I'll have a roommate, too. Dany will be staying in there with me."

"Well then, if the bed is too crowded, you can tiptoe across the hall to Wyatt's bed."

Was it possible for a person to instantaneously combust? At that moment, the heat that enveloped her body made her feel as if it were possible.

Jax laughed, turned, and headed back to the elevator without another glance.

Inhaling and letting her breath out slowly, she walked into the conference room. Gaige sat at the conference table; a large screen came down from the ceiling at the far end of the room. He had a computer on the table and a conference box sitting toward the middle of the table.

He turned to see her walking in. "Yvette, come and sit here so Max can see you."

Biting her bottom lip, she stiffly sat at the table next to Gaige and looked at the screen. There was nothing on it right now, but she didn't know where else to look. For some reason, Gaige made her nervous.

Gaige rose, walked to a refrigerator across the room, and pulled out a bottle of water. Bringing it back to the table, he set it in front of her, then started explaining who she'd be talking to.

"So, Max is the assistant to our contact at the State Department. The State Department is in charge. Our contact with the military, Casper, doesn't like his identity revealed, so I'm afraid it's all a bit cloak and dagger. Casper reports to our State Department contact who calls the shots ultimately. Both of them have their own contacts to assist us such as with "friendlies" who are police or local law enforcement who get us out of jams. Sometimes Max and Casper do it themselves."

Nodding, she didn't know what to say so she opted for silence.

The conference box on the table began ringing and she jumped.

His intense gaze landed on her and held. "You okay?"

Nodding, she took a drink of water to wet her throat and watched as he tapped a few keys on the computer.

"Max, how are you?"

"Doing well, Gaige and how about you?"

"No complaints. This is Yvette Jacobsen. Yvette, Max."

"Yvette, thank you for agreeing to meet with us. I want to assure you we will do everything we can to keep your name out of this, but Caulfield will likely know you gave us information."

Stiffly she sat up. "I understand. But he has to be stopped."

"Okay, let's begin with the basics..."

She answered the usual questions, her name, where

she worked, how she met John. Then onto the more
serious questions and her stomach rolled.

"Tell me why you feel complicit in his activities."

"We would go out to this one hotel he liked called the
Bismark. He'd see a young woman usually trying to look
older, walk into the hotel bar and he'd ask me to go chat
with her. At first, I didn't understand and didn't want to do
it, so he grabbed my arm and told me to do it a few times
before I did. Every time we were at the Bismark, I had to
chat with them. I see now that he was using me to keep
them there while he had one of his thugs come and get
them."

"What makes you say that?"

"He'd always be texting while I was chatting with the
girls. Like he was ignoring us. But just as we'd leave, a man
would walk in and they'd nod at each other. That was it,
just a nod." She took a deep breath and blinked rapidly as
moisture gathered in her eyes. "I didn't know what I was
doing, but that doesn't change that I did it."

"Why did you do it?"

"I was afraid of him. He had a temper. He was also very
good at talking me into things."

"How did you find out what he was up to?"

Gaige sat quietly alongside her; and even though she
was nervous around him, his presence made her feel
better. Calmer. Protected.

"The first girl I chatted with appeared in a news
bulletin I saw on television a while later that she was
missing. John saw it when he came out of the shower and
turned off the TV and chewed me out for watching it. I'd
had enough and I told him it was over and walked out."
She fidgeted in her chair, cleared her throat, and continued. "He charmed his way back into my life and I

stupidly took him back. Activities soon resumed at the Bismark. If I'd ask a question, he'd get pissed. I thought it was weird, so I snooped while he was in the shower and found a password list and log in information in his phone. Then, the night before I got into his account, I pretended that my username and password wouldn't work on my laptop and asked him to try to log in. He was reluctant but I told him I needed to order his favorite shower soap on the internet. Since it was about him, he didn't hesitate then. The next day he was going away. I didn't know where or for how long. I logged onto my laptop as him and checked his emails. I scrolled through and found a few that gave me an idea of what he was up to. Dates, times of pickup. Deposits of large sums of cash into his bank accounts. Then my phone rang shortly after I logged off, and it was him asking if I'd logged onto his email account. I freaked out and lied and said no, how could I. But I immediately booked a flight and began packing a bag."

"Did you happen to see any locations of where an exchange might happen?"

Looking at the table she thought through the emails she'd seen. "Oh, one!" she exclaimed. "He said, the second location I75 314."

Max and Gaige at the same time began typing into their computers and Max looked up at her from the screen. Gaige said, "Bushnell, Florida."

"That gives us a basic area to begin scoping out."

Gaige then leaned forward. "Caulfield is here in town. I saw him yesterday; I'll email you the pictures of the car he's in. Rented."

Max typed into his computer, then looked back at her. "Do you know how long he's been doing this?"

Regretfully shaking her head, she responded. "No, I'm sorry."

"How about names of any of the women?"

"The first girl he wanted me to talk to was Lola. She looked like a Lola. She had blond hair and expectant green eyes. She was the woman on the television that was missing except in the picture of her, she had dark hair. The second girl was Jasmine. Darker complected, dark eyes, tall and slender. The third one was Julie. She had dark hair and blue eyes. Said she was from Ohio."

"That certainly helps us, Yvette. If there is anything else you can remember, let Gaige know and he'll get in touch with me. Thank you so much for helping us with this."

"You're welcome. You have to stop him. I lay awake at night thinking of these poor girls. They were all young. I don't know how he knew they'd be there at that bar, but it's weird that they would always show up. They always looked nervous and like they were waiting for someone."

"We'll certainly do our best to find out and your descriptions should help us quite a bit."

The door opened and she turned her head to see Wyatt enter the room with a gorgeous young woman trailing closely behind him. She looked like him in her coloring, but she was definitely much smaller. She smiled at him then, she was so happy to see him. It rather surprised her at how much she'd wished he had been here during this interview.

Gaige said good-bye to Max with a promise to email and then turned in his chair to face Wyatt.

When Wyatt only stared at her, Gaige cleared his throat and Wyatt's eyes then shifted over to Gaige's.

"Ah, hope we aren't interrupting, but I'm giving Dany,

a tour and wanted her to meet you. Dany..." His hand pointed in her direction, "This is Yvette and this..." His hand moved toward Gaige, "Is my boss, Gaige."

Dany stepped forward, a smile on her face. She was bright-eyed and engaging. "I'm so happy to meet you, Yvette. Thank you for inviting me here."

Without waiting for a response, she turned to Gaige, smiled radiantly and said, "Nice to meet you. You're the groom, right?"

Gaige smiled. "That I am. It's nice to finally meet you. Dany. I've heard quite a bit about you over the years and seen at least a hundred pictures not to mention a few videos."

"You have?"

Gaige nodded. "We all have."

Dany turned to Wyatt a smile on her face. "Really?"

The pink in his cheeks deepened and Yvette smiled. He was quite possibly the most handsome man she'd ever seen. Badass. Huge. And Smart.

and stepped

preceded him

"We can walk off our supper outside and I can show you the compound at the same time."

Dany reached over and took Yvette's hand and he thought how nice it was that they were getting along so well. He smiled as he watched them, these two women, [illegible] both of whom he felt strongly about. Well, strongly about Dany. Yvette, well, he liked her. He liked kissing her. He wanted to do that again. He'd thought about it every free second he'd had today. But they honestly didn't know each other that well.

He followed them down the four steps of the sweeping veranda. He then caught up to them with two long strides.

"I can show you the memorial trees in the back."

Yvette tilted her head up and he noticed several things at once. Her hair was gorgeous. Thick, long, brunette but the fiery hues where the sun shone on it were mesmerizing. Her frame was tall compared to Dany, but they were both slender. Her smile reached her eyes and the bruising in her face was fading with each passing hour. And she was simply stunning.

"Jax mentioned something about a tree planted for her dad and Jake and Dodge's son, Adam. And there's another tree planted by Sophie and Gaige for Kate and Tate."

"Yes, I noticed when she needs to reflect, she sits under the trees and the look on her face is always peaceful. So, the team bought a bench for her to sit on for her birthday this year. She was unusually quiet when we gave it to her."

Yvette laughed and it was a sight. "I'd love to see Jax rendered speechless by emotion. She's the strongest person I know and not much gets to her."

Nodding he only responded with, "Yep."

"I can't wait to meet Jax. She wasn't here at dinner, right?"

"No, she was feeling tired again today, so she went home this afternoon. She's married to Dodge and they have a house outside of town. At least I've heard, I haven't seen it yet." Yvette quickly answered.

Dany nodded and they walked silently for a few steps. What struck him was how comfortable he was in this silence. No one seemed nervous or chatting wildly to fill it and he rather liked it.

They wound around the side of the house to the back and Yvette sighed. "It's simply like magic here. I feel safe. It's beautifully kept and yet we're close to town."

"All by design. Gaige was very precise in what he wanted for us here and he makes sure it's maintained that way, too."

He stopped just before the trees and stared at them. They were beginning to bloom for the spring, and the sight of the new growth was refreshing.

"Wow, this is gorgeous." Dany exclaimed.

She walked forward to the bench and read the inscription on the plaque on the back, then turned to the trees. Little plaques at the base of each tree named the type of tree, the date of each person's death, and the date the tree was planted.

"Oh, Adam was only four years old when he died."

He nodded and cleared his throat, "Car accident."

"Oh, how sad."

She didn't need to know the rest of the story, but clearly, Yvette knew. She looked up at him, a sad smile on her face, waiting for him to explain, but he had no intention of telling his daughter that Adam's mother was driving drunk and Adam was killed because of it.

Yvette reached over and took his hand, lacing their fingers together and squeezed. He looked into her eyes and saw the special hazel of them, the thick lashes framing them, her clear skin, her beautiful smile. She almost seemed too beautiful to be true. If he told himself the truth, even their hands felt good locked together as they were.

Dany leaned down and used the hem of her bohemian styled skirt to rub dust off each plaque and he couldn't help but think that was a Susanna thing to do. She cared.

Glancing down once more at Yvette, he squeezed her fingers with his, then said, "Should we go to the other side of the yard? I'll show you where Sophie is planning on setting up tables for the reception on Saturday."

Yvette released his hand and he felt lonely. Dany caught up to them and giggled. "I can't wait to see everything pulled together. The flowers and bows I saw earlier were so pretty."

"Wait till you see the foyer area all decorated. I'm a guy

and I even thought it was gorgeous when Jax and Dodge got married."

He led them to the other side of the lawn and watched Dany looking all around at the heavily landscaped grounds and flowers that did wonders to hide the tall wrought iron fencing surrounding the compound. He knew where the cameras were and could spot them with ease. But to the untrained eye, it would be impossible to see that Gaige, or any one of them for that matter, could pull up feed from the cameras and see who was walking around the yard.

Glancing up at one of the cameras, what caught his eye was the car that Caulfield had been driving earlier, slowly drive past on the back street. Peering through the shrubs, he actually saw Caulfield's smug disgusting face as he crawled on by.

"Okay, shall we go in and finish the inside tour?"

Dany turned to look at him and pride filled his chest. Never would he have dreamed he'd be partly responsible for making a human being like her. She was beautiful, compassionate, smart, and lovely to be around. She'll make a fantastic nurse.

Yvette looked up at him then at the street. She must have seen the car and Caulfield too because she instinctively tried shrinking in size and stepped behind his body. He turned to her, wrapped an arm around her shoulders, and began walking them to the house.

"It's okay. You're safe here."

Dany caught up to them, "Was that him? Did you see him?"

[illegible] to her [illegible] Wyatt's hand rested [illegible] his eyes assessed her

"You're safe here."

"But he's too close. What if he finds a way in? What happens if you're gone or busy? What happens if he..."

Wyatt pulled her to his chest and wrapped both arms around her. [illegible] Wyatt's body felt so strong, solid, and comforting against her. His scent swirled around in her brain, the firmness of his arms around her waist made her heartbeat increase rapidly. Maybe that was the fear.

"What's going on?" Sophie entered the foyer from the hallway and Dany responded.

"Caulfield drove by the back street when we were outside. It has Yvette rightly rattled."

She pulled back from Wyatt and looked over at Sophie. "I'm sorry I brought this here."

Sophie reached down to her ankle and pulled a gun

from her ankle holster. Checking the magazine, she dropped it down. Then satisfied with what she saw, she slid it back in and tucked it in her back waistband. Sophie then looked at Wyatt.

"Did you let everyone know?"

"Not yet we just walked in."

"I'll take care of it." Sophie's eyes then met hers. "You okay?"

All she could do is nod. That was unexpected. The soft, beautiful, happy bride was a tough, solid, hard-ass. It made her feel weak that she didn't know how to do that. Not even how to shoot.

As Sophie walked away, she tilted her head up and looked at Wyatt.

"I want to learn how to shoot a gun. I want to be strong. I want to be able to protect myself. I want that."

Dany spoke up then, "Me, too. That was probably the single coolest thing I've seen all day. Oh my God, I want to be her when I grow up."

Wyatt whispered, "Jesus."

Stepping back, he said, "Are you ready to tackle that right now? We can go down to the shooting range and have our first lesson. No shooting tonight, we'll practice holding a gun, loading the clip and drawing. We have plastic training weapons and you two can carry them around to get used to the weight of them, the feel of them and practice drawing several times a day. If after that you still want to learn to shoot, I'll train you."

Dany clapped her hands. "This is so frigging awesome."

"Dany, it's not for play."

"Oh my God, I know that. But clearly there's an

asshole running around that is pushing his boundaries and I want to be able to protect myself, too."

"Shit." He muttered then held his hand out toward the hallway and the elevator. She and Dany preceded him down the hall.

Stepping off the elevator on the conference room floor, he turned to the left and led them down a hall in the opposite direction of the clinic. Waving his card in front of a door that looked like all the other doors she was dumbfounded and amazed to see a room such as this.

They stepped into an interior room with lockers, tables, and a row of security vests hanging on one wall and cubbies on the other. Inside the cubbies were black cases and a team member's name on each cubby. Some of the cubbies on the bottom were labeled, "Training", "Miscellaneous", "Practice", and some were not labeled at all.

Wyatt stooped and pulled two cases from the "Training" cubby and set them on the table.

"You can tell this is the top of the case because the label is on the top." He pointed to an orange sticker on one side of the case. "This is the muzzle side. In other words, the muzzle is facing this way in the case. You never open this case unless the muzzle is pointed down range."

He turned the case to what looked like a row of windows pointing at a black room. Walking to the panel of light switches on the wall next to the door, he lit the room she was facing, and she saw a shooting range. She'd only seen one on television, but it looked the same. There were lanes, plexiglass panels in between each lane and at the far end of each lane was a target hanging. There were electronic conveyors above each lane and a counter at this end of each lane as well.

Opening the case, he showed them the muzzle and

then pointed to the lane. "If someone is in there shooting when you come down here, you take the case into the shooting range room, unopened, keeping the muzzle pointed away from any other human. When you get in there, you lay the case on the counter muzzle down range then open your case. Any questions?"

Both she and Dany, speechless shook their heads and he must have been satisfied as he continued.

Pointing to a button on the left side of the gun, next to the handle, he said, "This is the safety next to the stalk. When holding the gun away from you and anyone else around, you use your thumb to drop the mag from the stalk. At the same time, you never, never, ever, put your finger on the trigger." He rolled his wrist so they could see the other side of the gun he held. "Your finger always rests above the trigger on the side of the gun. You do not put your finger on the trigger until you are ready to fire. If I see either of you put your finger on the trigger any other time, these lessons will stop. That is the single most important thing you will learn today."

She whispered, "Okay."

Dany nodded her head and he continued.

He pulled the safety down slightly and the magazine dropped from the bottom of the stalk. He caught it in his hand and held it up to them. "This is where you'll practice loading the bullets."

Her stomach, while excited to be learning and feeling as though she was finally going to know how to protect herself in some significant way, still felt like butterflies were fluttering around. Her heartbeat was so fast she felt as though her whole body moved. This was what people must mean by "shit getting real".

[illegible] down, [illegible] and saw [illegible] from the bottom of the [illegible] although was careful with his knee because if he stretched it too far sometimes his knee cramped up on him.

Rolling slightly to his right, he lifted his phone and looked at the time. 7:00 a.m. He hadn't slept that late in [illegible]. Sighing [illegible] he [illegible] ran his hands down his face and stared straight ahead for a few moments before turning and dropping his feet to the floor. He walked to his bathroom he let out another sigh and did his business.

Exiting the bathroom, he pulled clothes from his closet, stepped into his black khakis, black short-sleeve t-shirt and boots. Stopping at his bedside table he grabbed his phone, wallet and gun then left his room while holstering it. He walked downstairs to see who was around as the fresh aroma of coffee filtered up to him and he inhaled heavily. This was a great way to wake up.

At the bottom of the steps he turned right, walked the length of the foyer to the back where the kitchen was located and entered, which was beginning to smell amazing. Mrs. James was at the counter whipping up something in a bowl.

"Good morning, Wyatt, did you sleep well?"

She was the perfect employee for them. She never asked personal questions, she never butted into GHOST's business. She was professional, polite, and incredibly good at her job. He guessed her at mid-fifties but only because Kylie, was nearing thirty.

"I did. Whatever you have cooking smells amazing."

She smiled, and he thought her husband was a lucky man. She was a beautiful woman, her short-cropped graying hair was always styled neatly, but no fuss, no muss. She remained trim and she gave off the aura of never getting overly excited about the stuff she had to do. Things like cleaning blood out of clothing, keeping bandages, aspirin, and other pain relievers well-stocked and dealing with their ever-chaotic schedules.

"I'm making a breakfast casserole this morning and I'm just now whipping up a cake for later today. Gaige's sister and her family will be here for dinner tonight."

He looked at her, then remembered the wedding would be held in a week and of course people would be coming and going. How would they manage the security of Yvette and the others while a steady flow of visitors would be in attendance?

Josh entered the kitchen just then sweaty from a workout and grabbed a coffee cup from the counter. Pouring coffee from the pot into his cup, he turned and looked at Mrs. James then him.

"Morning. Boy, Wyatt you sure lit a fire in Yvette. Shit,

she's been downstairs in the gun range practicing her drawing, loading, and unloading a clip for two hours now."

"What? How do you know she's been down there for two hours?"

"I let her down there. I took guard duty last night."

Nodding Wyatt filled his coffee cup, added a dash of creamer and took a sip of the hot aromatic liquid. He needed his coffee in the morning.

Lifting his cup by way of salute, he decided to see how much practice Yvette was actually doing. And while making his way down there, he tamped down the little green monster that was trying to climb up his back because Josh had been spending time downstairs with Yvette. It was just stupid to get worked up over it.

Entering the outer door of the gun range, he watched as Yvette pulled the practice pistol from her holster and pointed it at a target in the inner room. From this vantage point he could see her right forefinger was resting on the gun just above the trigger. Her drawing was pretty good, though a little clumsy, but she'd come a long way.

"You've been practicing."

She spun around and looked him in the eye. Hers were clear, crisp and as beautiful as he knew them to be. She smiled then and it caused his heart to skip a beat.

"Yes, I want to do this right and I want to do it quickly. John's too close."

Setting his coffee on the table next to Yvette he asked, "What time did you get up this morning?"

"Around 3:00 I think. I couldn't sleep anymore and if no one was around to let me in here, I would have practiced somewhere else. The dining room or something. I didn't want to wake Dany."

"I admire your dedication."

Her smile grew and they both stood still admiring the other. Stepping forward he lay his right hand on her left cheek; his thumb softly swiped her cheek and she turned her head into his hand. His heart thumped in his chest and he stepped closer. When she tilted her head up, his lips touched hers lightly. But that wasn't enough. He pulled a fraction of an inch away, but she leaned into his lips with hers and kissed him. It felt exhilarating.

Her fingers then wiggled through his beard and brushed the silky hairs down before sliding through his long hair until she reached the back of his head. He tilted his head slightly and his lips fully engulfed hers. The feeling of their lips locked together was something out of a dream. Hers were full and soft and oh so kissable. His lips wanted as much of her lips as they could get.

His hand slid to the back of her head and held her in place as his tongue began tasting, swirling, and enjoying her mouth. She tasted like cinnamon, she felt like heaven. His body responded almost instantly as his cock thickened against her lower belly.

Pressing himself into her as much as their clothing would allow, her left hand slid down to his ass and pulled him in tight. His heart raced, his body vibrated with energy, his breath became ragged. All this from a kiss. What would it be like to actually be with her?

it with her body. As he lay close and she got into the compound and as his body felt against hers. Thoughts about Wyatt won the war. As she lay awake in the darkness, hearing Dany's even breathing beside her, she envisioned Wyatt's body warm, solid, and so manly stretched out on his bed. Those thoughts made it impossible to get to sleep. It impossible to relieve herself of the tension that had been building the longer she was around Wyatt.

She'd never dreamed of John when they were apart. She never envisioned him making love to her in the quiet hours of the night. She'd known Wyatt for a few days, and she was thinking of him often. Many times, in positions that were better left to the privacy of the two of them alone. Kind of like right now. But she also didn't just want a fling. She wasn't a fling kind of woman. It would be hard to have to stay here and deal with him on a regular basis if they had sex once or twice and then he moved on. It would be humiliating, too.

Jax had warned her that she still had to work with Wyatt, and they would continue to be friends. Yvette had to admit there would be an awkwardness between them and she didn't want that for anything. Jax was her only girlfriend that she could always count on. Pissing her off or driving her away would be like cutting off her own right hand.

Wyatt began maneuvering them to the corner of the room. In her head she knew she should stop their movement; she knew what would happen when they were secluded in the corner. The feel of his rigid cock between them had made her nipples pucker a while ago. The wetness between her legs was another sign that her body responded to him in ways she struggled to remember with another man. He was massive. Tall. Broad. Smart. Strong. Alpha. Sexy. For God's sake, what wasn't he?

His left hand slid around her rib cage, so gently it belied logic that this enormous man could be so tender. Then she felt the pressure on her nipple, the slight tug, the pinch between his thumb and forefinger and his cock pulsed between them.

A shiver ran the length of her body. A vibration throbbed through her and landed between her legs and her knees weakened. His lips never stopped moving against hers and her mind became blank, refusing to allow her to remember if she'd ever been kissed like this. Did that mean never? Somewhere in the fog, she thought it did.

In an instant she felt the wall at her back, and she was lifted. Her legs instantly encircled his waist and her arms wrapped around his shoulders. She'd lost her mind a while ago. Her body had taken over and there was no thought process at all. Just the spicy fragrance that encircled her and grew as his body heat increased.

The feel of his muscles bunching and stretching under her had her body more ready than she'd ever been and she couldn't have stopped this now if she'd wanted to.

His voice washed over her as he ruggedly whispered. "I've thought about you all night. You are sexy. You always smell fantastic. Your hair - my God, I love your hair. Then I kissed your lips. Haven't fucking thought straight since then."

She shivered at his words. The huskiness in his voice showed his need.

She managed a few words. "I've thought about you, too. I've never met anyone like you."

She felt the instant his hand pulled her yoga pants down around her ass; the coolness of the air against her warm skin was exhilarating. Before she could say or do anything, a large finger slid into her wetness and she gasped. She pulled away from his lips and kissed along the side of his face, enjoying the feel of his beard against her cheek. She dipped her tongue into his ear, and she was rewarded with a second finger inside of her and that alone almost made her cum. She gasped, then moaned, and his fingers massaged in and out as far as he could manage with her pants in the way.

"Set me down," she ordered, and he wasted no time.

Quickly pushing her pants down her legs and stepping from them she was pleased to see that he'd unzipped his black Dockers, slid them down his slim hips, and pulled his cock forward as he massaged it with his right hand. Something shiny caught her eye and she froze.

"You have a PA?"

"Yeah. Does that bother you?"

"No." She swallowed but couldn't look away from it. Mesmerized by the silver bar at the head of his penis and his thumb, which now roamed over it. "I don't know. I've never..."

He hefted her up quickly and she felt the cool wall behind her back. His fingers again found her wetness and pumped in and out of her a few times.

"You're so fucking wet."

"Yes." She couldn't say anything more. She was both excited and nervous about how he would feel inside of her.

"Ready?" His voice was gruff and told her more about his excitement than anything else.

"Yes," she managed. All of her senses were now trained on where he pulled his fingers out and placed the very broad head of his cock. She could feel his pulsing and warmth, but he hesitated.

"Yeah?"

She pulled back and looked into his eyes. The beautiful amber orbs were so focused on her. His lashes were impossibly long. The fine lines at the corners a sexy statement to a life well lived. He made no move to enter her, so she wiggled on top of him. He dropped her down just a fraction, so the head of his cock was now inside of her. He then slowly pushed his hips forward as he dropped her down onto the length of him and she closed her eyes to focus solely on the feel of him entering her. It did not disappoint.

He filled her completely; the tightness of the way they fit together was something she'd never felt before. It was almost as if he was too big, but her body wanted so badly to accommodate him; she felt the acceptance as he then pulled his hips back and slightly raised her up with his strong arms. Repeating that movement over and over again they found a rhythm together, him entering her then pulling out and her legs tightened and loosened to help him hold her.

She wanted him, all of him, the feel of his piercing could be felt slightly but she couldn't be sure if it was the piercing or him. His size, just him.

They worked together as both of them began to sweat, their breathing heavy and choppy, their bodies straining for more. She felt like a wild animal, she wanted him all the way inside of her and she pushed herself down to drop further onto his cock and enjoyed hearing his grunt and felt his hips raise up as their tempo increased and the beats they shared became more possessive and wild.

He pushed her firmly into the wall and dropped her down a fraction as his right arm then shifted pulling her left leg up higher just as she dropped down on him again and she felt herself slide further and him go deeper and her body shivered.

"Again." Her plea was almost desperate, but he felt the same way, she saw it in his eyes and the grin that instantly formed on his face and he repeated that move. His eyes closed and so did hers and she willed her orgasm to hold off because this feeling was - everything. She wanted it to last.

"Oh my God...so good."

"Yes. Fucking...fantastic," he managed.

He pushed roughly into her twice more before grinding out, "You gotta get there, Ette. I'm..."

She tightened her legs once more and the flood washed over her as she cried out, "Wyatt. Oh...fuuuck."

"Yes " he hissed and pushed roughly into her and froze as she knew he spilled into her.

...to the [...], her heart still beat rapidly. She [...] was smiling. And though they'd just finished having sex, he wanted her again. Now. It hadn't dimmed his desire.

She gently took his hand and he looked down into her eyes. They almost glittered now. Sparkled. Her lips were beautiful swollen from his kisses and her cheeks were flushed. Her pulse was still beating rapidly in her neck.

"That was amazing," she whispered.

He squeezed her fingers. "It was."

They stopped in front of the elevator, but instead of waving his card, he turned to face her.

"So, I'm not...Do you need..."

Taking a deep breath, he was relieved when she laughed.

"I don't need hearts and flowers and all things perfect, Wyatt. For some reason, I can't think of anything more perfect for our first time than the spontaneous, wild, hot passion we just shared."

Bending down he kissed her lips softly.

The elevator door slid open. "There you ar..."

He turned to see Dany staring at them. "Hmm, I see things are a bit more than 'friendly'," she used air quotes, "with you two."

Quickly he said, "No."

But Yvette said, "Yes."

They looked at each other for a moment then Yvette turned to her and said, "Um, no."

At the same time, he said, "Yes."

Dany wasn't fooled and his cheeks flamed a bright red. "So, which is it?"

Not sure where to go from here, he looked down at Yvette and waited for her to answer. They hadn't talked about how they would play this. Whatever this was.

Yvette smiled at him and he couldn't help it, he smiled at her. She positively glowed. Then her cheeks tinted a pretty pink and he thought she was simply gorgeous.

Her fingers squeezed his hand, and she turned to Dany. "We're not sure what is between us at this time other than to say there is a strong mutual attraction. I hope that doesn't bother you, Dany and I don't want to take away any time between you and your dad. You're here to get to know him better and he you. That said, I hope to get to know you as well. And if Wyatt and I do move forward together, it's my hope it will be with your blessing."

Stunned would be a good word for his feelings right now. That and he couldn't have said it better. He turned to face Dany, cleared his throat, and nodded.

"That's cool," Dany responded then jumped in quickly with, "I need to go shopping. Skye and Roxanne said they'd go with me. I don't have a dress for the wedding. Yvette, do you want to go, too?"

"No." His voice boomed causing Dany to flinch and Yvette to jump. "It's not safe for Yvette. And, Dany, I'd be much more comfortable if someone went with you for protection. At least until we get Caulfield off the streets."

Dany's brows furrowed and he realized he'd undoubtedly pissed her off or embarrassed her. Plus, he made a decision for Yvette he likely shouldn't have made. But it wasn't safe. Especially for Yvette.

"Who should go with us? Do you want to go?"

"Shopping?"

"Yes, shopping."

He scraped his hand through his hair and swallowed the cotton ball that had formed in his throat.

"Ah, shit. I hate shopping."

He pulled his phone from his pants pocket, scrolled with his thumb, and found Jax's number. Tapping her picture, he held his phone to his ear.

"Hey, can you go with the women shopping today? They need protection."

She almost yelled it. "Shopping?"

"Yes, shopping."

He grinned when he saw Dany's grin. He'd used her words after all. Then he thought he was going to get an earful, so he tapped the speaker icon and let Dany and Yvette hear Jax's response.

"I hate shopping. Is Skye going? She could shop all damned day. "

"I understand Skye and Roxanne are going."

"Oh, for fucks sake. Both of them could moonlight as marathon shoppers."

Dany spoke up then. "And me, Jax, it's Dany. I need a

dress for Sophie and Gaige's wedding. I didn't bring anything. Please come with us."

"Fuck," Jax muttered.

Yvette giggled and Jax heard her. "Ette, are you going, too?"

Yvette looked up at him, her cheeks still pink but the mischievous look in her eyes was interesting.

"Yes, I'm going. And I haven't been shopping in such a long time that shopping with two professionals sounds fantastic. We could start out at the dress shops and make our way through jewelry, then on to lingerie. We could make a whole day of it and maybe have lunch and dinner somewhere before finding the perfect pairs of shoes to go with all of our outfits."

"I am not doing that. Nope. I hate shopping. I especially hate shoe shopping. And I'm still so frigging tired I couldn't make it a whole day."

Yvette moved closer to his hand holding the phone, and the mischief on her face was replaced with worry. "Jax, I think you need to see a doctor. Honestly, this is so not like you to be tired all the time."

Jax let out a long breath. "I know. Dodge just gave me that lecture and I have a call into my doctor for an appointment. I can go shopping for just a couple of hours, and only if you all promise not to make me shop or try on clothes. I'm just there for security. Is that a deal you can live with?"

Yvette looked over at Dany and Dany nodded her approval.

"Dany just agreed and I won't be going today. Wyatt feels it isn't safe for me and to be honest, I'm a bit afraid to leave the compound now with John circling."

Jax was quiet for a few moments. "Ette, Wyatt will keep you safe, I promise. Besides, I'll kill him if he doesn't."

Dany giggled then, "Oh, he's keeping her safe a_right."

"Do tell."

"I just caught them kissing." Dany smirked at both of them and his damned cheeks burned. The little chit was going to get her digs in.

"Hmm. Well, then. It seems you two are getting along."

Dany's grin said it all. Precocious little imp. Yvette nudged him with her elbow, and he looked down to see her smiling at him.

He shook his head to clear it. "Thanks, Jax. What time should I tell the women to expect you?"

"I'll be there in an hour. Make sure they know the rules."

The line went dead, which meant Jax was finished with this conversation. She'd taken the news about him kissing Yvette well enough, and actually what could she say? She'd told them her thoughts on things, and that was that. They didn't need her permission. That didn't mean she couldn't make it tough on them, but he doubted she would. It wasn't Jax's style to do that. She'd just tell them off and move on.

"Okay ladies, let's go upstairs and get Skye and Roxanne rolling."

29

Yvette scooped a ... onto her plate. ... her plate and her cup of coffee into the dining room. She found a seat at the table where Roxanne and Hawk were sitting.

"Are you going shopping with us this morning, Yvette?" Roxanne asked.

Looking up at the silver haired beauty Yvette smiled. "No. We weren't this bitter free. Dani is going with you and Skye and Jax will be here in an hour to go with you as security."

Roxanne smiled. "I love tormenting Jax while shopping."

Hawk chuckled and leaned back in his chair. "Poor Jax."

Dany came in and sat beside her. "Jax said she's still tired though and we can't stay out all day."

"I'm worried about her. She's the most vivacious woman I know. It's not like her to be tired all the time." Roxanne added.

Yvette took a sip of her coffee. "She has a call into her doctor to make an appointment."

Roxanne leaned forward, "Yvette, do you have something to wear for the wedding? We can shop for you if you like."

"I'd love it if you don't mind. I skipped town so fast I didn't pack a variety of clothing items, and I don't have anything dressy with me at all."

Wyatt came in and sat alongside her and without a word began inhaling his food. She glanced over at him and noticed Hawk doing the same thing. Dany giggled beside her and Roxanne looked at Wyatt then her. Her eyebrows rose into her silvery hair in question, but Yvette wasn't going to get into anything personal with her. Likely Dany would fill them all in while they were shopping, which made her heart race a bit faster.

She didn't know Wyatt all that well. What she knew she liked. Really liked. But they hadn't known each other that long and it was difficult because living here in the compound, the daily stressors didn't exist as they did for real world couples. If they were a couple at all. She had enough to deal with just worrying about John and how long could she hide out here. She'd have to find a job soon enough; she'd run out of money and all her belongings were at her apartment. Shit her apartment. She'd have to give notice soon because she couldn't afford it. Plus, John knew that place too well, so she'd never feel safe there anyway.

Suddenly her appetite diminished, and she felt foolish for filling her plate so much. Her stomach lurched at the thought of all she needed to take care of and maybe that was the best course of action right now. She'd spent the past few days not thinking about moving forward but instead hiding in her safe bubble here. She really did need to be responsible about her future. The word responsible made her flinch. They'd just had unprotected sex, which was anything but responsible. But she was still on birth control, so that was a worry she didn't have.

She set her fork down and picked up her coffee cup.

Roxanne leaned forward on the table. "When you're finished, let's go upstairs and figure out your sizing, then I'll be prepared to shop for you. Dany, will you help me pick out an outfit for Yvette today?"

"I certainly will. It'll be fun." Dany then turned to face her, that playful smile again on her face and Yvette knew something sassy was about to pop out of her mouth.

"What should I look for something wedding appropriate or lingerie?"

Yvette choked on her coffee and Wyatt choked on his breakfast. Hawk smiled and sat back assessing both Wyatt and her. Dany smiled ear to ear and Roxanne gave her a knowing smile, then sat back as her husband was and grinned.

Before either she or Wyatt could say a word, Skye and Lincoln entered the room. "Morning."

Skye looked around the room at each person, then looked at Roxanne. "What's going on?"

Roxanne laughed. "I think Wyatt and Yvette are going on."

Lincoln laughed, then walked around the table with his plate of food and sat with a chair between him and Roxanne. Skye sat in the empty chair at the table and took a bite of the breakfast bake before setting her fork on her plate and looking over at Yvette.

She chewed daintily and took a sip of her coffee. Yvette's body grew warm, a trickle of sweat slid down the back of her head and she was grateful no one could see it. She had to fight the urge to run and hide. Wyatt's knee touched hers under the table and she looked up into his face. His expression was unreadable, and she wasn't sure if she should say something or not.

He set his coffee onto the table, looked at Hawk and said, "Go ahead. I believe you owe me after I gave you shit about Roxanne in the beginning." Then he looked at Roxanne. "Let's get it over with."

They were saved by Jax walking into the dining room. "I see everyone already knows about Wyatt and Yvette. You people are unbelievable. Remind me to play cards with all of you; your faces are so easy to read."

Dodge walked in behind Jax, a wild grin on his face, he kissed Jax on the back of the head and sat at the far end of the table.

Wyatt looked down the table at Dodge, "What's the big grin on your face for?"

"What, a guy can't be happy? Sheesh." Dodge's hair was still damp on top as if they'd left home straight from the shower. He patted the chair next to him and looked at Jax. "Come on, little mama, take a seat."

Jax walked to the end of the table, sat next to her husband and said, "Here are the rules for today. We're only going to three stores. Get what you need. We're not looking at furniture, housewares, linens, makeup, hair products or anything else. Dresses, shoes, and that's it. I want to be home for lunch. Got it?"

[illegible] ference room [illegible] told him the whole [illegible] ing out" scenario was largely over. He'd asked Yvette before heading down here. She was heading upstairs to give her thirty-day notice on her apartment and to call her office about the possibility of working remotely.

Gaige was seated at his computers and Wyatt sat next [illegible]

"That bad?"

"Naw. There's just a lot going on and I'm trying to figure out how to handle it all. Dany came to spend time and get to know me better, but now is off shopping with the women. Yvette..."

Gaige chuckled but to his credit didn't say anything.

He sat quietly watching Gaige organize his files and video, then Gaige looked over at him.

"You wanna see what we have here?"

"Yes." He watched as Gaige rolled down the large screen from the ceiling with the push of a button and projected the same video on his computer onto the screen in front of them.

"Caulfield has been driving around regularly. I'd say he's rightly worried. He parked in the back and got out of his car a couple of times to check out the fencing. I suspect he's planning something."

"Fuck." Wyatt watched the video of Caulfield, getting out of his car, looking the wrought iron fencing over, shaking it to see how sturdy it was, looking for places where it could possibly be breeched then getting into his car, and driving away.

Their wrought iron fencing was eight feet high, pointed at the top and sturdier than hell, the only way he'd be able to breech it was to use explosives.

"He's rather regular, too. Every couple of hours, all night long. He always seems to be alone and slows down to see what he can see. Then around 3:00 this morning, I noticed this."

He tapped a couple of keys on his computer and a video was shown on the screen.

"Caulfield got out of his car this morning and attached a device to the front of the gates." Gaige reached over and picked up a small electronic device from the top of his desk and lay it in front of him.

"It scans codes continuously looking for the code to enter the property. It successfully found the first two and was continuing to scan. Luckily for us, our software changes our codes after every use, so these numbers that device found were only good until the gates were used again. But I've just changed that so that the device changes the code every ten minutes."

"Son of a bitch, he has balls and access to high tech equipment." Wyatt watched Caulfield walk to the gates with the small device in his hand, turn it on and attach it to the code box on their gates.

The smarmy look on Caulfield's face enraged Wyatt.

Gaige glanced his way once, then back to the screen. "I imagine the thought of going to prison has him very worried."

"Hanging around here isn't going to keep him from going to prison."

"No, but people like him would likely want revenge and the risk of getting caught is diminished by his need to exact his punishment on Yvette. We've seen this over and over."

"Right." Scraping his hand through his hair again Wyatt continued to watch the various videos of Caulfield to see if something was amiss.

"I've already sent these to Casper who has likewise forwarded them on to local authorities. Now that he's stepped on our property and attached a device to try to break in, they can move forward with detaining him when they find him."

His phone chimed a text at the same time Gaige's did and they both quickly looked at the messages received.

"Dany taken from the back of Leonard's Clothing. I've got the other women." The message from Jax sent a lump of lead plummeting into his stomach.

"Caulfield has my daughter," Wyatt yelled.

Gaige quickly sent a text to the other members of the GHOST team.

"Need someone in the Beast to pick up the women at Leonard's Clothing. Dany missing."

Almost immediately Josh responded, "On it."

Within a minute Hawk, Dodge and Lincoln entered the conference room, sweating from their workouts in the gym with looks of pure hatred on their faces.

"That fucker harms one hair on any of the women, he's definitely toast," Dodge threatened.

Wyatt's fingers flew over his phone as he rifled off a text to Jax.

"Did you see anything?"

"No. Chatting with the store manager now for video. Gonna need help with this."

Wyatt looked over at Gaige. "Need the video feed from the store. Jax says she needs help with it. The manager must be asking for a warrant or something."

Gaige turned and looked at Lincoln and Dodge. "You got this?"

Neither man said a word they just turned and left the room. One thing he knew for sure, this team would do whatever it took to get Dany back.

Wyatt stood and moved toward the door. "I'm going up to talk to Yvette. She may know some of Caulfield's habits and give us some idea of where he may have taken her."

The elevator seemed slower for some reason and his heart, it felt like it was breaking. Then a surge of anger burst through him; anyone, no matter who, that would be so bold as to touch a hair on his daughter's head was a dead man. And why Dany? She's young. He must have followed them from here. Didn't Jax notice anything? How did he get Dany out of the store without any of them noticing? The questions wouldn't stop coming at him. The dread he felt of what Caulfield might be doing to her consumed him. He had to stop Caulfield before he could sell Dany, too.

team table with Gaige. All the team members were searching the area and obtaining the video from the store. Thank God there was a gas station across the street with video. Casper had called local authorities to obtain the video and it was currently being uploaded to the GHOST computers. Wyatt and Josh were looking at the video at the gas station now. If she'd have been with them she could have taken her and not Dany. She should have been there. She should be where Dany is now wherever that is. Now, she felt numb.

Gaige's fingers flew over his keyboard since he had placed some tracking on John's phone he hoped he'd be able to locate it.

"Got it." Gaige turned to her; his eyes bright with excitement. "It looks like he's just about 65 minutes out of town at a house owned by Bennet Martin. Does that name mean anything to you?"

"Yes." Her brows furrowed as she tried remembering

how she knew this name. "It's his grandfather's name I think."

"What are the fucking odds he'd have family here?"

She shook her head. "I didn't think he did. I'd never have come here if so. I can't believe..." She looked up at Gaige, her brain felt fuzzy. "He's dead. I thought he said his grandfathers were both gone."

"Gone as in dead or just out of the picture?"

Shaking her head, she had to tamp down the anger she felt with herself. "I don't know. I think he said gone and I assumed dead. When he said gone, I believe my response was that I was sorry. He chuckled and said, it's not that bad or something."

Gaige turned and began tapping away on the computer again. The door opened and Sophie entered the room nodded at her then went to Gaige.

"What do you need me to do, babe?" She asked as she sat in front of the computers next to Gaige.

"Look for a death record for Bennet Martin. I'm looking for real estate records. We might find something useful."

She watched them work side by side, their fingers flying over their respective keyboards and she felt inade-quate. The least she could do was help them as much as possible. Worrying about Dany was eating at her. Worrying about Wyatt and his feelings about her responsibility in the disappearance of his daughter just made her feel like she was drowning with no way to come to the surface.

"Minnesota." She blurted it out without thinking and Sophie turned to look at her, her beautiful brows bunched together.

"John flew to Minnesota on business often, as in weekly."

Sophie nodded and Gaige turned to stare at her. "Do you know if he flew into Minneapolis?"

Nodding she responded. "Yeah. Minn Minn he said. Minneapolis, Minnesota."

Gaige and Sophie then turned to each other and a knowing glance passed between them. Sophie then turned to her. "Minneapolis is the trafficking capital of the US right now."

Her eyes watered as all the conversations she'd over-heard about Minn Minn came flooding back to her. Then she jumped up and sat next to Sophie.

"His emails mentioned ads." Sophie's eyes locked on hers and held. To say Sophie was beautiful was a clear understatement. Actually, all of the women here were model worthy. Sophie's dark hair and dark eyes were stunning. Her smile made her jealous of her beauty and the way Gaige looked at her, well, that was swoon worthy.

"As in one of those sale sites?" Sophie asked.

"I think so. Try Carl's Site."

Quickly turning to her computer Sophie typed furiously and soon a site populated showing listings categorized by type then lists appeared on her monitor. Without prompting, Sophie clicked on "Job Listings" and found some ads. Quickly scanning through them she found a search icon to be able to focus her search on areas and she typed in "Florida". One by one jobs appeared, the list was long, but Sophie then filtered them by customer service. A few ads were filtered out and Sophie clicked on a few.

"Son of a bitch. He's putting ads on the internet for Customer Service Reps needed for in-person hostessing. Dirty fucker is calling trafficked women hostesses."

Gaige stopped what he was doing and read the ad on Sophie's monitor.

"Hostesses needed for all shifts to meet and greet guests and help them acclimate to the area. In person interviews only. Apply with the link below."

Sophie clicked on the link and an application popped up. She filled it in using a fictitious name. Then she was to upload a photograph and without hesitation she uploaded a picture of herself as a teen.

Gaige opened his mouth to object, but Sophie cut him off quickly.

"I look the same but not. And this is a good picture of me, he's likely to respond."

She clicked send and Gaige sat back in his chair with a look of dread on his face.

"Soph, don't put yourself in danger like that."

"I believe he'll respond. He's in the area and I said I'm from Indianapolis. Far enough away to feel safe for him, yet close enough that we can set up a sting. At a minimum, we can track him back to where he's staying and maybe find Dany."

"You will not get in the car with him."

"Why not? I'm capable of defending myself. I have the benefit of knowing what he's all about and finding Dany."

"Soph, we've talked about you putting yourself out there."

"You've talked about it. But I'm an operative of GHOST and I'm the perfect person to do this. Jax gets all the fun and I want in. Plus, Dany."

Her computer pinged and she smiled. "See, he responded already."

She clicked on the link and a message popped up.

"I've reviewed your application and would like to set

up an in-person meeting. When can we meet? I will be in Indianapolis this evening."

Her fingers flew over the keys before Gaige could respond. "How about 7:00 tonight? Where should we meet?"

"Hotel Aton just off of I-80. Wear a dress, the hotel is formal. I'll watch for you."

She smiled at Gaige. "I'm in."

... the back of ... from Leonard's ... blood boiled. He saw Caulfield's car exit the parking lot of the store and Dany with a gag in her mouth and fear in her eyes. There was someone else in the backseat with her.

Josh said, "His accomplice is a new addition, at least, to this area. We need to see if Yvette has seen this man."

Wyatt pulled his phone from his pocket and called Gaige.

As soon as Gaige answered Wyatt said, "Pull up the video and look at 10:37. There is someone in the backseat with Dany, see if Yvette knows him."

"Will do."

Then Josh quickly said, "Stop the recording." The attendant tapped the button and stopped the surveillance recording. Josh leaned in closer. "Back it up a couple of seconds."

The attendant did as asked and Josh sneered. "She was

in one of the dressing rooms. That dress she has on has the security tag hanging off the neck in the back."

Wyatt leaned in and saw the tan plastic security tag hanging from neckline of Dany's bright pink dress.

"She had on a white t-shirt and jeans this morning when they left."

Josh pulled his phone from his pocket and tapped a couple of times before putting the phone to his ear.

"Jax, she was in one of the dressing rooms. Is there a backdoor by the dressing rooms?"

Josh listened a minute then turned to face him.

"There's a door in the back of the dressing room Dany was in, which Jax had them open. It's an employee exit area to a smoking patio out back."

"Fuck." Wyatt snapped.

"Okay. Get everyone to the Beast. We'll be out shortly."

The attendant turned in his chair and looked at Josh. "Anything else you need?"

"No, the video is already uploaded to our server, just make sure you don't erase this one. Thanks."

The attendant turned. He didn't look much more than 16 years old. He was eager to help and very good with the equipment. He shut down the video, removed the portable hard drive from the computer. "I'll put this in the safe."

He had a sheepish grin on his face, then said, "You Jax's twin?"

Josh looked the attendant in the eyes and smirked.

"You know Jax?"

"Fuck yeah, she's badass as hell. And hot."

"She's married, you know."

"I know. I've seen her husband. I'd never want to mess with him."

"Right." Josh chuckled then walked out of the tiny room.

Wyatt glanced at the attendant and nodded. His temper was still at an all-time high and saying anything at this moment was likely to get him in trouble. He wanted his daughter back. He wanted the piece of shit who called himself John Caulfield off the fucking streets and he wanted the women that asshole had sold safe.

Walking across the street to the Beast, he climbed in the very back through the liftgate and tapped the button to close the door. Sitting at an angle so he could stretch out his legs, he stared out the back window.

His phone chimed that he had a text and he pulled it up to read the message.

"Sophie has made contact with Caulfield through a Carl's Site help wanted ad. She's meeting him tonight in Indianapolis and we'll be there to follow him back to wherever he's staying and hopefully find Dany. The video is too grainy for Yvette to identify the man even after we cleaned it up."

"Wyatt? You get the text?" Josh asked from the front seat.

"Yeah." He yelled back. He typed in a reply. "On our way back."

Using the time in the back of the Beast, he closed his eyes and tried clearing his mind. To finally have the chance to get to know his daughter and she to know her father only to have her taken forever could not be the way this ended for them. Tyler would be so devastated, too. He was torn between letting her know what had happened and waiting till it was all over. Of course, afterwards, when they got Dany back, Tyler would be mad and demand to know why he hadn't let her know. But she'd get over that once Dany was safe and back home. Right now, there was no sense in worrying her. Plus, he didn't need her calling him repeatedly asking him what was going on when he was on this mission. What a fucking shit show. And he was wrestling with being pissed at Jax. She was there to protect the women. What the fuck was she doing not watching Dany? Goddammit all anyway. As if she knew what he was thinking, she turned to him from the backseat and quietly said, "I'm sorry, Wyatt."

"Where were you while she was being taken?"

"I was standing not far from the dressing rooms watching Skye and Roxanne. I thought Dany was safely trying on clothes in a dressing room. I had no idea there was a door, which, by the way, no one knew about except the employees; it was a hidden door. An employee took a $100 payoff to let that asshole in through said door."

Scraping his hand through his hair, he heard Josh from the front seat issue a stern, "Not now." But he couldn't help wondering why Jax hadn't checked the dressing rooms before letting any of the women go in there. It was so unlike her.

Turning his head, he saw Josh look at him in the rearview mirror.

Roxanne sat next to Jax in the backseat. Skye was in the passenger seat up-front. Everyone was heads down texting and he assumed they were texting their husbands, who were rightly both freaked out and worried by how close call Caulfield came to them.

Taking a deep breath, he turned to stare out the back window and calm himself. He worried about how they were going to get Dany back. Then he shifted gears and started thinking in his most effective manner as a GHOST operative. Using his head was what he had to do now.

Texting Gaige, he asked, "Do you have a plan?"

"Working on it." Was the reply he got. Then another text quickly followed. "Meeting in the conference room as soon as you get back."

"Roger."

Wyatt knew this would be the most important mission of his life.

watching ... of walls was both ... and interesting.

"Sophie, we need to talk about this. First of all, I get that you're excited to be in the thick of it, but we're getting married in a few days. Finally, after all these years we're getting married. And, dammit, Soph..." He walked to her and framed her face in his hands. "I can't lose you. Do you understand what I'm saying to you?"

Sophie's smile was soft, understanding and meant to convey empathy, but her words cut right to the chase.

"I understand that I mean as much to you as you mean to me. Everything. But part of who I am, who we are, is that we sacrifice to help those who need it."

Sophie turned her dark head, her high ponytail swooshing with her movement. "Yvette needs our help and all those women Caulfield has sold into sex slavery need our help. I no more want that for myself than I do for any other woman. But if we're going to try to have a child, what if that child is a little girl? Would you want this kind of scum out there on the streets to potentially prey on her? What about Dany right now? Wyatt is likely going out of his mind."

Gaige stared into Sophie's eyes. His even sparkled with moisture as they filled with tears. Rapidly blinking them away he closed his eyes and lay his forehead on Sophie's. Yvette thought she'd never seen anything so beautiful in her life. It was at that moment that she knew what she wanted out of life. She wanted that. Someone to love her like Gaige loved Sophie and vice versa.

She also wanted to be that. Someone who would sacrifice herself to ensure that someone else would have a chance in life. It was surreal like a light switch had just turned on in her brain and the last 36 years of her life seemed to mean nothing. But the next 36, if she had them, would mean something totally different. She'd do whatever it took to use her values to be a champion for others. Like the members of GHOST. Someone who protected others instead of being someone to be protected.

Gaige kissed Sophie's lips and hugged her hard. Then Sophie turned to her.

"Yvette, tell me what will get John's attention. Short dress? Hair up or down? What will make him want to take me tonight to wherever he has Dany?"

Gaige's groan from behind Sophie was loud but Sophie ignored him.

"Sophie, I don't know that he took Dany to sell her like the other women. I also don't know what happened to the other women after we left and his henchman came into the bar to, I assume, take them."

Sophie came to sit at the table next to her. "What did they look like?"

"Young. Lost. Scared. It's as if they got on a plane to

meet a stranger for a great opportunity, then realized they were in a hotel bar meeting a stranger, who likely had nothing but misery for them. And then they were ready to bolt. When I think on it now, they usually looked scared shitless and that's when he'd have me to chat with them. Like he was afraid they'd leave before Ira or whoever could get there."

Gaige asked, "Who's Ira?"

Yvette looked up at him, her brows pinched together. "John's friend, the dirty cop."

Gaige began typing on his keyboard and Sophie reached across the table to her hands, which lay there, and squeezed them.

"Hey, you aren't responsible. And we're going to get that son-of-a-bitch. And Dany."

Yvette's eyes welled with tears, one escaping and sliding down her cheek. "Is there any way I can ask you to change your mind that you'll listen to?"

Her head shook before words came out. "Look, I'm trained. I'm smart. And..." Sophie turned to look at Gaige, who turned and stared at Sophie as if he were trying to memorize this moment. "I have everything to come back to. I won't fail."

Yvette squeezed Sophie's fingers and nodded. "Okay. I understand and I believe you. And you do have everything to come back to. We should all be so lucky."

Sophie stood, turned and gave Gaige a sweet soft kiss on the lips, then said, "I'm going up to get ready. I assume by the time I'm ready, you'll have a plan in place and certain weapons for me to use?"

"You know that for a fact, Soph."

Sophie exited the conference room and Yvette stood.

Timidly she asked Gaige, "Is Axel still here? I'd like someone to show me how to shoot a gun."

"You can text him; he's programmed into your phone." Gaige turned to the computer screen, tapped a couple of keys, then said, "I've given your card access to the gun range. Don't make me regret it."

"I promise I won't. Thank you."

She texted Axel who responded a few minutes later. "I'm just finishing up grabbing supplies. Come on down to the range now."

Both nervous and excited, Yvette left the conference room, leaving Gaige typing furiously away on his computer. Images of the hotel where Sophie was to meet John tonight populated the screen. She knew he was scoping out the area and making his plans to keep his love safe. She'd be doing the same thing tonight to ensure both Sophie and Dany were safe. Hopefully, in the end, she'd be safe as well. But if not, she'd leave this earth knowing she did what was right, and she'd helped someone else. And those thoughts alone made her feel like she could fly. She got it now; how these people felt about helping out others and putting their lives on the line. It was exhilarating.

feeling since he first started life felt meaningless and somehow wasted. He'd had a daughter whose mother had died. Instead of spending his life raising and loving this little girl, he'd given her to his sister, who couldn't have children and loved her with her whole heart. But he'd left Dany believing he didn't want her. It was just the opposite. He didn't even think he was a whole person; how could he raise a daughter?

Now, just when they had the chance, evil befell her, and he'd do whatever it took to get her back whole. And this was what he was good at. He was certain that all of his years prior to this were training for this moment. No one could tell him otherwise and he'd move heaven and earth to make sure he didn't fuck it up.

But first, he wanted to talk to Yvette because for some strange reason the thought of sitting with her for a few minutes was the only thing that he needed to put his head completely on straight and get ready for this mission.

He stepped inside the elevator quietly. Waiting for the rest of the group to enter and stand in front of him tried his patience. His eyes met Jax's once and he quickly looked away. He couldn't quite make out his feelings about her right now. She'd always been one of the best operatives they had. This was simply not like her to let something get past her. Plus, she was a friend.

The ride up was quiet and the doors whooshing open seemed loud by comparison. Jax, Josh and he stepped off the elevator leaving Skye and Roxanne to continue on upstairs. He knew he was to report to the conference room, but when Jax and Josh walked in that direction, he pulled his phone out and texted Yvette.

"I'm back. Where are you?"

It took a minute, but her response was a surprise when she texted back, "Gun range."

Pivoting he headed in the direction of the gun range. He was surprised to see Axel walking out a grin on his face. "She's not bad for a beginner."

"What the fuck is that supposed to mean?"

Axel chuckled. "Easy, bro, she asked me to help her learn to shoot."

Ducking his head, he stalked to the gun range. As he walked in, his mind flooded with memories of this morning and making love to her in this room. His eyes darted to the corner he'd maneuvered them to and his body responded to the flashbacks.

Hearing shots from the inside range room his eyes turned to see Yvette standing in the far-right lane shooting 15 feet from the target and doing pretty damned good. Her shots all concentrated around the middle of the target, and while not perfect they were consistent. She emptied her clip, dropped it from the gun, and pulled the slide back. Then she looked inside to ensure the chamber was empty, lay her gun on the counter before her and turned to see him standing there.

She walked to the door at the same time he did and as soon as the door opened, the smell of gun powder, gun oil and Yvette slammed him at once. He scooped her up in his arms and held her close. When her arms wrapped around his neck and her face nestled close to his ear his eyes closed.

"I'm so sorry, Wyatt."

Emotion flooded through him and his voice refused to work. His nose stung, his eyes filled with tears, and his heart pounded in his chest. What felt right at this moment was to hang onto her.

Her legs wrapped around his hips and his arms snaked around her body tighter, but not as tightly as he'd like, she had on a bulletproof vest, which was bulky. Holding each other for a long time, he finally loosened his grip and her body slid down until her feet touched the floor.

Taking her hand, he pulled her to the outer room and sat on the table where usually they lay their weapons while putting on their vests. She sat alongside him, her eyes assessing his.

"Are you okay?"

Her concern caused his eyes to well again and he tamped down the weakness that sprang forth. Blinking rapidly then swiping at his eyes he took in a cleansing breath and nodded.

"I'm going to get her back."

"I have no doubt. For what it's worth, everyone here feels it, too."

"These people have been my family for ten years most of them anyway. I have no doubt they will do what it takes to get her back."

Yvette leaned forward and took his hand in hers. "Jax is kicking herself for not checking the dressing room before-hand. She had no idea that back room existed and she's mad as hell at herself."

He scoffed and shook his head. "She's been my friend and teammate for a long time, but I'm struggling with my feelings on how to handle this right now."

Yvette scooted closer to him, her fingers sifted through his beard, gently touched his scar, and her warm breath fanned across his face.

"I can't tell you how to feel about Jax. All I know is she's angry with herself which is worse than anyone else being angry with her. She'd cut off her right arm rather than endanger anyone she loves, or anyone that person loves, and she loves you. She knows Dany is everything to you and she let you down. "

Her clear tawny eyes stared into his. She stood and moved herself to stand between his legs, her lips softly touched his. Too quickly her lips left his and her arms wrapped securely around his neck. His phone vibrated and he knew he was being summoned, but he just wanted a few more seconds with Yvette. Her lips kissed the shell of his ear, and he heard her intake of breath, breathing him in as if to commit to memory before she whispered, "You're being summoned. Don't worry, we'll get her back for you."

He squeezed her again, then moved to stand kissing her lips once more.

"I'll see you in a while."

"Take care of yourself, Wyatt. You'll be no good to Dany if you get killed. Or me."

"I'll be careful."

He hugged her tightly one more time. His heart felt better when she returned the gesture and his mind calmed. It was too soon to know yet and not the right time, but he wanted to explore these new feelings he had for Yvette. It was a feeling he hadn't had in all the years since Susanna had died. A reawakening of sorts.

"When I get back, we need to talk."

She smiled at him though it looked sad. But she stepped back as she said, "Of course."

Something about her tone made his gut twist again, but a text came in again and he knew he had to go

35

She had been […] the clip into the […] in the holster she wore. She closed the lid on the gun case and tucked it into the cubby she'd pulled it from. She'd need to borrow the gun for a while and, since these were all practice guns, no one would be the wiser for the time being.

Pulling her t-shirt down over the gun, she walked out of the […] to the elevator. The team was in the conference room and she wanted to make it to her room without notice. Stepping inside the elevator she held her breath till the doors slid closed then let it out.

To say she felt responsible for Dany's kidnapping by John was an understatement. Dammit all anyway, for being so weak she was unable to protect herself. Never again. Even if tonight she died, she would go out making amends for everything John had done and she, innocently or not, had taken part in. There was comfort in that.

The elevator came to a stop on the second floor and she exited quickly and made her way across the hall to her door. Waving her card, she slipped inside unnoticed, pulled clean clothes from the dresser, and locked herself in her bathroom. Undressing, she started the shower to warm the water, lay her gun on the floor in the corner with her dirty clothes over it so it wouldn't get wet, and rapidly stepped into the shower. Her knees and elbows were still sensitive but healing and the water only mildly stung as it hit them. Washing her hair, she made the rest of her plan. By the time her shower was finished, she felt a peace and calm settle over her. It was going to work.

Dressing in the only pair of jeans she'd brought with her, she attached the gun holster to the belt of her jeans and drew her weapon a couple of times to check her ability to do so. While she was still a bit clumsy with it, she knew she could do this.

Finishing her outfit with a dark blue t-shirt, which concealed her gun, she smiled and exited the bathroom to don her tennis shoes.

Brushing her hair out and gathering it at the top of her head, she tied it in a ponytail, secured it with a band, then wound the tail around the band and slid in a few bobby pins to hold it all in place. Since John was fond of grabbing her hair, she hoped this would keep him from grasping it, and so stopping at least one of his methods of controlling her.

Picking up her phone she searched for a car service, called them, and asked to be picked up in an hour. All she had to do was wait for the GHOST team to leave, then she'd walk out of the gates and meet the car down the street. This just had to work. It was the only thing she could think of to help Wyatt and Dany. She knew Wyatt needed Dany for his life to matter. Pulling money from her purse, she pocketed what she had in her front pocket.

The thought of Wyatt caused summersaults in her gut. He'd be mad at her for what she was about to do. And damn she wished she would be here after Dany was rescued so she could explore a relationship with him. He seemed as though he was interested in getting to know her better. The sex would likely be hot as hell based on this morning. He was passionate but sensitive. If things were different, she'd chase him all over the world if that's what it took to have him for her own.

Isn't it strange that now that she knew she had to sacrifice herself for him, she wanted him more than she'd ever wanted anyone in her life? Her feelings for him no doubt started as soon as she saw him. She'd been scared to death by his size, his scar, and his tattoos. Once Jax vouched for him, she became intrigued. But as he showed his many sides, she'd fallen in love a little bit each moment they'd spent together. Figures love would find her now that she knew tonight she'd be the property of John Caulfield. Given her age he wouldn't sell her, but, without doubt, the coming days would be nothing short of hell if she didn't kill him first.

Hearing the motors running, she looked out her window to see the Beast exit the gates. Another vehicle, which looked exactly like the Beast, followed right behind it. Inhaling a deep breath, she let it out slowly, closed her eyes, and made peace with her decision. Then, she opened her bedroom door, and quietly walked to the elevator.

The ride down was quiet, the air felt thick, though that was probably her imagination. On the main floor, she walked to the front door, opened it quietly, and slipped outside. Once she reached the gates she held her breath as she waved her card. She didn't know if Gaige had given her access to the gates, but when it clicked open, a sigh escaped her lips. She slipped through the opening hurrying down the street to the corner where she was to meet the car service.

Keeping her eyes alert, she watched every car that drove past. Luckily, it was a smaller town and there wasn't a ton of traffic to worry about. Her phone vibrated and she looked down at it to see her car service alert that the driver would be at her destination in three minutes. The driver was in a white Prius.

Looking down the street, she saw the car and watched it near her. It came to a stop and she looked at her app before climbing in to confirm the driver was the man in the picture the service had sent her. As soon as she sat in the passenger seat, she told the driver, "I need to go to Hotel Anton in Indianapolis."

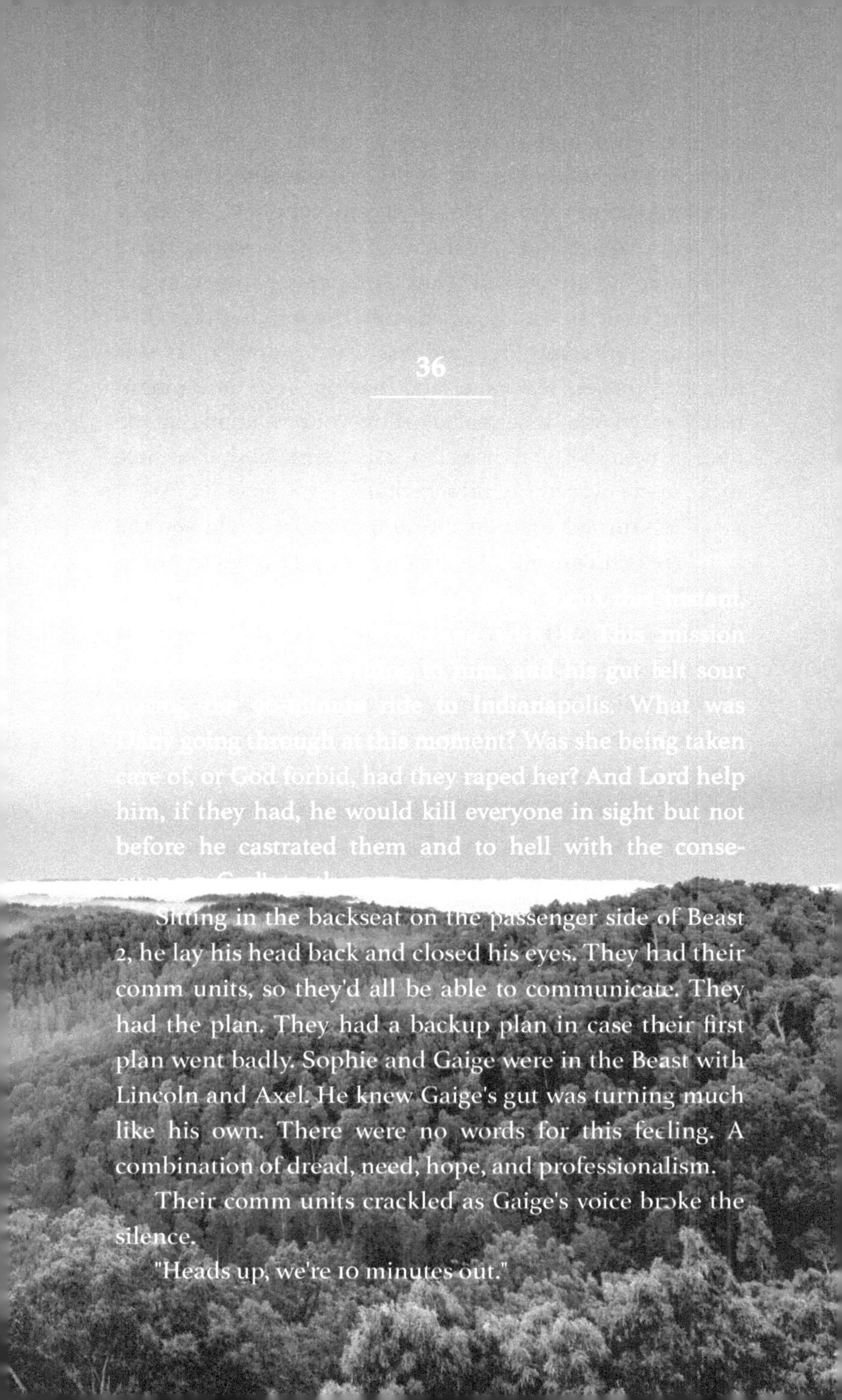

important. This mission ... to him, and his gut felt sour ... six-hour ride to Indianapolis. What was [Isaty?] going through at this moment? Was she being taken care of, or God forbid, had they raped her? And Lord help him, if they had, he would kill everyone in sight but not before he castrated them and to hell with the conse-...

Sitting in the backseat on the passenger side of Beast 2, he lay his head back and closed his eyes. They had their comm units, so they'd all be able to communicate. They had the plan. They had a backup plan in case their first plan went badly. Sophie and Gaige were in the Beast with Lincoln and Axel. He knew Gaige's gut was turning much like his own. There were no words for this feeling. A combination of dread, need, hope, and professionalism.

Their comm units crackled as Gaige's voice broke the silence.

"Heads up, we're 10 minutes out."

Josh, Ford, and Dodge were with him in this vehicle. Dodge drove while the rest of them began checking their weapons, comm units, clothing, and supplies. He knew the other vehicle's occupants were doing the same. There was a comfort about it all. They'd prepared before they got into the vehicles, and it got them in the mindset that they were on a mission. Preparedness was a necessity as was focus. Mindset, the plan and having your equipment ready to go was essential. Feeling your weapons at the ready, mentally preparing to use them, and complete focus made everything gel together.

They turned onto an off-ramp and he could see the hotel signs up ahead. The area wasn't very large or populous. There was a gas station on the right, a larger hotel on the left and the Hotel Anton's sign shone only down the road about another half of a click to the left.

He swallowed the lump in his throat, took in a deep breath, and set his mind on getting his daughter back come hell or highwater. His eyes landed on the men in this gargantuan SUV with him and he knew they'd all been in similar situations. They'd do anything for him, each other, and Dany since by way of him she was one of their own. That made him feel better. If it came to it, he knew they'd die for her. Hopefully, it wouldn't come to that.

They drove past the hotel and parked in the lot of the vacant tractor dealership next to the hotel which was out of sight behind the building. The instant the SUVs were parked Gaige's voice crackled over their comm units.

"Axel and Dodge in the back. Wyatt and Josh, front. I'll be on the West side of the bar inside. Ford and Lincoln East side of the bar on the inside. Jax, you copy?"

Jax the sound of her name made his stomach flip. He

had to get over that. She'd apologized over and over. Because of the tension and the fact that she didn't feel well, she was back at command monitoring communication and any video feed they had, Hawk was there too, in case Jax needed a break, she'd not been feeling well lately. Gaige had patched into the hotel camera system earlier thanks to a sweet little gadget GHOST's contract hacker and computer genius, Jared, had sold them.

"Copy. I have eyes on the lobby area and the entrance to the bar. Caulfield is inside the bar as of two minutes ago."

"Copy," Gaige responded. "Get in place. Sophie will be inside in five minutes. This goes down smooth - copy?"

They each responded to Gaige and moved to their places. Josh would be inside the lobby area reading a paper. He would then walk to the Beast once Gaige hopped out and take it to the front of the Hotel. Driving into the parking lot, he spotted Caulfield's car. It wasn't a well-traveled hotel apparently, only about 5 cars were in the parking lot tonight. Probably why Caulfield chose it.

Dodge was moving Beast 2 into place near the back.

He watched Josh walk through the front door and one by one his teammates called quietly over their comm units, "Set" as they were in place.

His heart pounded and his eyes darted between Caulfield's car and the front door.

Sophie appeared from the edge of the parking lot. Her long, dark hair was flowing in curls down her back. She wore a short red dress and high black heels. She'd always been gorgeous, but tonight she was a knockout. She had a gun in her purse, a knife strapped to her upper thigh, a knife attached to the underside of her heels and a small pistol between her breasts in a bra holster. Gaige was taking no chances that she wouldn't be armed or caught off guard.

She walked with purpose; her head held high. And as soon as he could no longer see her as she disappeared inside the building, his heartbeat ramped up to the point it was slightly painful.

Jax's voice sounded low and calm. "Sophie's in the bar."

A comm unit toned and he heard Gaige's voice. "I'll take a bourbon, neat." That was confirmation that Gaige was in the bar.

He waited glancing at Caulfield's car then back to the front door. Lincoln's voice sounded over the comm unit. "Two beers, whatever you have on tap is good."

Ford and Lincoln were in the bar. The waiting was the worst part. Always the damned waiting, but this time the minutes crawled by agonizingly slow. He knew it would take a while. Lincoln then came over the comm unit nice and low. "Sophie's chatting with Caulfield at a table. No accomplice.

That's when he noticed the man, who looked suspiciously like the man who had been in the back of the car with Dany, get out of a white Impala. He walked toward the door his head turning back and forth. The look of a guilty man for certain. He wondered where Dany was if both men were here. His breathing hitched. What if they'd already sold her?

He warned his colleagues. "Accomplice entering the hotel."

Ford responded, "Roger."

Lincoln added, "Caulfield on the move alone."

He put the Beast in gear in case he had to follow but what he'd rather do is block Caulfield in and check out the accomplice's car to see if Dany was inside. Where else would they leave her?

"Accomplice with Sophie."

He saw Caulfield walk out of the hotel texting on his phone as he walked. He was likely making a deal to sell Sophie this moment. It was perfect, he wouldn't even notice them. The urge to kill him this instant was almost overwhelming. But if he did, he may never know where he took Dany. Restraining himself at the moment would be the hardest thing he'd ever do in his life with the exception of rescuing Dany.

Caulfield got to his car and slid into the driver's seat. The glow from his phone was still visible.

"Jax," he called. "Caulfield is on his phone. Can you see what he's texting? Gaige has his phone hacked."

"Hang on," Jax responded.

Gaige's voice came through, "Accomplice with Sophie exiting the bar."

Jax answered, "I can't get the message."

Wyatt got out of the Beast and walked to Caulfield's car. Glancing in at the phone he saw the words "prime," "top shelf," and "$50,000."

The fucker was making a sale right now.

He stepped back so he wouldn't be seen and backed up to the Beast. Climbing into the driver's seat, he saw a car pull into the parking lot and drive around the perimeter. It drove up on the far side of Caulfield's car, then stopped relatively close to it.

He saw an iPad being handed to the passenger and then handed back. The passenger door opened and his heart damned near fell out of his chest.

Yvette stepped from the car and it sped away. She turned to look at Caulfield's car just as accomplice and

Sophie neared the white Impala. Yvette kicked Caulfield's car and Caulfield jumped out.

Calling on his comm unit he yelled, "Yvette just showed up and is confronting Caulfield."

Gaige replied, "Wyatt, stay the course. Do not approach and blow our cover."

Yvette looked at Caulfield. "John, take me and give Dany back. I'll go willingly as an exchange. But it has to be an exchange."

Caulfield sneered at her. "You really think you're in a place to negotiate?"

"I do. I've told no one what you've been up to, but if you don't give Dany back, I've got an email that will auto send in a half an hour to the State Police and to the Human Trafficking Task Force with all of the information I have. I can stop that from being sent, but I'll only do it if you give Dany back."

"You fucking little whore."

Yvette didn't flinch and his blood was boiling. Why would she do this? He could feel his teammates around him even though they stayed hidden. His mind was in a state of disbelief. He needed to get Dany back. But he couldn't lose Yvette either. They'd just found each other. This could not be happening.

"You can call me all the names you want after the exchange, but I'm dead ass serious John, 30 minutes."

The accomplice told Sophie to get in the car and she ignored him. He tried to encourage her to get in by placing a hand on her upper arm and she shook it away. Caulfield looked over at his accomplice, and yelled, "50k."

The accomplice then grabbed Sophie by the arm firmer and tried to forcibly move her. She resisted and he got angry. He slapped her hard across the face, her head spun and before she could recover, he'd opened the front passenger door and shoved Sophie in. The accomplice slammed the door, ran around to the driver's side, and got in. Within a second, he had the car started and pulled out of the parking space.

____

even though she ... let him know it was ... Wyatt wanted to be with him so bad, but he had a chance with Darcy now. And she hoped she could escape from John or whomever she was sold to, if she was sold, someday. Then, maybe then, she and Wyatt would be able to find their way back to each other.

Training her eyes on John, she watched as indecision flashed across his face. Javier, who she thought was only John's friend apparently was his accomplice as they walked out, had taken Sophie and hopefully someone was tracking them.

"Time's ticking away, John. I'm not bluffing you on this."

She rolled her head from side to side to ease some of the tension. "Also, the cops will be swarming this parking lot as soon as that email goes out. I have them on call."

John's phone vibrated. He looked at the text he'd just gotten, then laughed and turned his phone around to show her the text.

"Your Dany is on her way to being a sex slave. So, you can see you no longer have any bargaining power."

"How will you collect your money from a jail cell?"

Her voice shook slightly, she swallowed, and admonished herself. She needed to be strong; he might be lying. He was.

She could see Wyatt's shoulders stiffen. His muscles bunched and twitched as he worked to keep himself from losing it. What would happen if she went with John now? Could she find something out? Could she figure out where Dany was and get word to Wyatt? Good God, she wished Jax were here to tell her what to do.

While reasoning this all out, she needed to make something happen here.

"Okay, you come with me, stop that email from being sent, and I'll take you to Dany."

"Not good enough." She saw one of the GHOST SUVs leave the parking lot and knew they were following Sophie. At least they were on that part of it. But she knew there was a second SUV somewhere in this parking lot. She didn't want to give up any hope they'd be following her.

"Alright, you little bitch, I'll take you to where Dany is and show you she's still alive, then you have to stop the email."

"I'll stop the email as soon as you let Dany go."

Her knees were beginning to shake, and she hoped like hell she could pull this off. Otherwise, both she and Dany and maybe Sophie were all lost. This couldn't be how it ended for her; it just couldn't be. Gaige would move heaven and earth to get Sophie back. There was no doubt in her mind about that. Plus, Sophie was badass and tough. Smart, too. So, she had hope again.

"Fine. Dammit. Get in the fucking car."

"Nope, I'll wait here."

John's patience disappeared. He yelled, "I don't have the fucking time, you stupid bitch. You think I have her here in the hotel? God, you're a stupid cunt."

She was proud of herself for not flinching when he yelled. In the past she would have.

"I'll follow you to where you have Dany."

"No, you fucking won't."

"It's the only way, John."

With lightning speed John pocketed his phone, reached out and grabbed her by the upper arm in one fell swoop. He pulled something from his pocket, and she felt the sting and jolt of what her mind assumed was a Taser.

She dropped down to the pavement. The bite in her knees from the landing caused her to cry out. Well, between the pain and the surprise of what just happened she was amazed she didn't pass out. Before she knew what was going on, he was dragging her to the car. He hit a button on his key fob and opened the trunk. She couldn't comprehend what was happening until he lifted her under her arms and tossed her in the trunk. The lid slammed without hesitation and she was engulfed in darkness. Her ears rang, her head throbbed, and her heart beat so hard and fast she thought it would jump right out of her chest.

She prayed Wyatt was near and would follow them or she'd gone through this for no fucking reason at all. She'd have done nothing to help Dany. She was not superhero material.

Rolling to her side, she felt the gun pressed into her hip and hope rang out once again. She pulled the gun from its holster and held it in front of her. Once he stopped the car and opened the trunk, she'd shoot this motherfucker. Lucien had Sophie and Dany and they'd have to take their chance with him and John's cell phone to figure the rest out but the Beast was following him so GHOST would find where Sophie and Dany were being held.

Taking a few deep breaths, she tried forming her plan. It helped to sooth her. She could do this. She could save herself, and Dany and Wyatt would be proud of her.

Pulling the slide back to engage a bullet in the chamber of the pistol, she held it close, and her finger just above the trigger like Wyatt and Axel had told her so she didn't accidentally fire it and kill someone. In this case, she didn't want to alert John that she had a gun. She tried counting in her head how many turns they took and in which direction. It wasn't working well because she was praying to God that He would help her, and that Dany and Sophie were safe. She prayed that He would help her do what needed to be done. Briefly she wondered if she'd go to hell for praying that she could kill John. She sent up a silent prayer that He understood that killing him was necessary to save who knew how many women from a life of slavery. She prayed that He would forgive her. Feeling a bit better about her situation, she felt the car turn onto a bumpy road, then heard gravel crunching under the tires and knew she needed all of her courage now. The car came to a stop and just for a bit of luck, she kissed the side of her gun. "Don't let me down, baby."

38

Wyatt, Bishop and Axel jumped into the Beast and he took off after Caulfield.

Reporting to Gaige and crew he said, "Caulfield has Yvette in the trunk. We're following at a distance."

"Roger. I have eyes on Sophie and his accomplice."

Jax joined in their conversation. "Lucien Montalbo is his name. Also, Yvette must have taken one of the practice guns because the tracking device on it is beeping and I can see where it's going."

Gaige responded, "Send the location to our phones so we have it. How about the tracking on Sophie?"

"Sophie is just ahead of them a few miles and it looks as though Caulfield is headed in the same direction."

"Keep eyes on them, Jax, good work. We're all enroute," Gaige finished.

Dodge's voice sounded, "That's my girl."

Lincoln and Ford in Beast 2 with Dodge smiled at him.

Wyatt took a deep breath and continued to keep his

eyes on the road and the car Caulfield was driving. For the first time, in a very long time, he sent up a few prayers that this would turn out the way he hoped it would. He also silently admitted that he likely didn't deserve it, but they did.

"Sophie has stopped at a house just outside of a town on Bulldock Road. It's the one in the name of Bennet Martin," Jax informed them.

"Keep tracking them, Jax," Gaige said.

A minute or two later Gaige pinged their units. "Okay, we're outside of the house. We've parked across the road and hid Beast 2 behind a house. I'll let you know when Caulfield pulls in. We're surrounding the house to get the lay of the land."

Axel responded for them, "Roger."

Caulfield was driving faster than he should be but not so fast that he'd get stopped by a cop. Wyatt didn't want to drive too close and spook him. Now that they had a good idea of where they were going, he simply kept his speed steady and his thoughts on the mission. Axel began giving directions.

"I've got the address on my phone now, Wyatt. Take a right off Bluemound Road about three miles up ahead."

His heart began to settle now that they had directions and he didn't have to watch for Caulfield. He just had to keep his mind on the task at hand. He tapped his comm unit.

"Jax, is Caulfield still heading toward the house?"

"Affirmative."

Relief began to settle in and Jax spoke again, "You're only about eight miles out now."

He glanced at Axel's phone, which Axel held out for him and he could see the clear directions.

Gaige broke the few moments of silence that had settled over them.

"Dany's here. It looks like they've drugged her. She's in an upstairs bedroom, on the bed, out to the world."

"Roger." His voice cracked as he tamped down the emotion. Josh's hand squeezed his shoulder from the backseat.

"We're going to get them all back, Wyatt. Today is a good day."

Tears flooded his eyes and he blinked them back. Swiping his face with the back of his left hand he took in a deep breath and let it out slowly.

"Caulfield is here."

Axel reached up and pointed to the exit up ahead and Wyatt took it. At the bottom of the exit, he took a left and followed it further out of town. Nearing a residential area, he crawled along the street until Ford spoke.

"I see you approaching. Turn left in five feet and park behind the house in the alley. We're across the street. We've still got the house surrounded and Lincoln climbed up the pergola post to see in the upstairs window, he's still there watching Dany."

A gunshot rang out, then another, and he heard Ford yell, "Motherfucker."

Then there was nothing. Turning quickly, he parked the Beast, and they jumped out, and silently made their way across the street. He saw Dodge helping Yvette out of the trunk of the car and a body on the ground behind it. Without knowing for sure, he felt the body had to be Caulfield. Ford reached over, took the gun from Yvette's hand, and then began to lead her toward Wyatt.

When they were within a couple of feet of him, Ford

nodded. "Take Yvette to the Beast and stay with her. We've got Dany and Sophie."

Yvette faced him tears streaming down her cheeks and blood spattered on her pale face.

"I killed him."

Wyatt pulled her into his body grateful to be holding her close again and memorizing the way she felt against him. He loved that feeling. The way they fit together. The way she smelled. The way she held onto him like he was the only person on earth she wanted to hold on to. Her body shook as he held her.

"I'm proud of you, Ette. You're a badass."

His voice was soft, he almost crooned into her hair.

She gulped in air and giggled lightly. "I'm so not, I was scared shitless."

"We all get scared when faced with the uglier element of life. But you did what you needed to do."

Gunshots rang out and she jumped in his arms. Tightening his hold on her he held his breath, praying that his daughter, Sophie, and his teammates were all okay. Nothing to do but wait and see at this point. He began walking Yvette to the Beast, so they'd be ready to get out of the area as soon as his team had Dany and Sophie.

The minutes ticked by with no sound. He was starting to panic about Dany. Feet crunching on the gravel reached his ears. Turning to see who it was, he saw Lincoln with a woman draped over his shoulder quickly making his way toward him. Wyatt stopped and waited; Yvette still clung to him like he was her lifeline. Lincoln stopped just in front of him and nodded.

"She's alive just drugged. I'll drive while you tend to her and make sure she's okay. Gaige has Sophie."

to the Beast. [illegible] the door then ran [illegible] Opening the hatch, he climbed inside and reached for Dany's limp body as Lincoln carefully placed her on Wyatt's lap.

Lincoln closed the hatch and Yvette looked back at Dany's face as the dome light faded quickly.

Stretching back, she lay her hand on Dany's forehead [illegible] back and listened to her heart. Reaching inside the bag he opened a plastic case and began assembling items: individually wrapped alcohol pads, a hypodermic needle, a small bottle of something. Pushing the short sleeve up Dany's arm, he opened an alcohol pad and cleaned an area in her upper arm. Inserting the needle into the clear little bottle, he tipped it up, loaded the syringe to a level he wanted, removed it and tapped it a few times, and then set the bottle down. Pushing the plunger of the syringe until some of the clear liquid squirted out, he squeezed Dany's arm where he'd cleaned it, pushed the needle in gently, and emptied the syringe into her arm.

Dany's eyes opened not long afterward. Her hands framed her face as she looked frantically around to get her bearings.

"Take it easy, Dany. You're safe, we're taking you back to the compound."

"Dad! What happened?"

Yvette watched as Wyatt's eyes stared into Dany's. She'd called him dad and he was visibly moved. He hugged her close to him and her arms wrapped around his body and hugged him back.

"You were kidnapped, drugged, and we just went in and took you back."

His eyes met Yvette's and held. "Yvette helped us get here. Sophie, too."

The doors to the Beast opened and teammates began climbing in.

Lincoln sat in the driver's seat. "Are we ready to go?"

Wyatt answered first, "Yes."

Dany sat up, though there wasn't a lot of room for both of them in the back with all of the toolboxes and weaponry. Wyatt maneuvered around so he was facing the back of the SUV, Dany faced him and the front of the SUV.

Yvette reached out, and ran her fingers into his hair, massaging his scalp. He responded by laying his head back against the seat his face looking up at the roof of the vehicle. Unable to resist, she leaned forward and kissed his temple and lay her forehead against his. His right arm came up and his hand reached up and held her head close to his.

The Beast began moving and she was grateful they

were finally on the move. Lifting her head, she looked at Dany.

"You okay?"

Dany nodded and smiled. "Yeah. You?"

"Yeah."

She turned and stared straight ahead. Axel sat next to her. Josh in the front passenger seat turned back and nodded at her.

"Jax said she's proud of you."

"Tell Jax I was trying to channel her."

He chuckled, relayed her message to Jax then faced forward. The Beast was quiet again.

Her guts twisted inside. She'd killed John. Even though he was a monster, he was a human being, sort of. He had no remorse for what he was doing and the women whose lives were destroyed because of his actions, they would likely disagree that he was human. When she got back to the compound, she'd see if she could get a private moment with Jax or Wyatt to find out what might happen to her for the murder. Then, she wondered why they didn't have to wait around for police.

Turning to Wyatt, she asked that question. His head still rested on the back of her seat, but he turned it to face her.

"Gaige will get it sorted for you, Ette. He likely already has but, if not, we'll get it straightened out when we get back."

"Okay."

She turned and sat back again resting her head against the seat back close to Wyatt's and stared straight ahead. Somewhere along the close to 90-minute ride, her body settled, and she fell asleep. The movement of the Beast slowing and turning woke her, and she sat up and looked out the window to get her bearings. The Beast turned once more and began its descent to the underground parking garage, and she felt safer already.

After Lincoln parked the Beast, they began to get out of the vehicle, each of them looking sapped of energy, exhausted, and prepared for the debriefing.

Axel opened the hatch and helped Dany out, and Yvette walked to the back and waited as Wyatt scooted to the edge and then dropped his legs to the ground. He paused for a few minutes and she locked eyes with him.

"Are you in pain?"

"Not really."

"What can I do to help you?"

He chuckled, "Loaded question. Ette."

Dany turned. "Eww."

Axel and Josh chuckled and walked to the elevator.

Wyatt stood, his arm immediately snaked out and pulled her close and there was nowhere she'd rather be than right here right now. Burying her face into his chest, she wrapped her arms around his waist, and enjoyed a moment in his arms. His other arm snaked out and he pulled Dany into their bodies.

"I love you, Dany." He whispered.

Dany tiredly replied, "If I ever doubted it, and I have, I never will again, Dad."

They stood for a moment more before Dany pulled away. She tiredly called out as she walked to the elevator behind the others, "Come on lovebirds or the elevator will go up without you."

Yvette giggled into Wyatt's chest and she smiled when his chuckle rumbled through his body. Now off to see what would happen to her for surely murder came with consequences.

his arm

arm around his

"When we get upstairs, I want to look Dany over in the light to make sure she's come around fully and to talk with her about what she can expect as to side effects from the drugs so we can all be aware. I also want to talk to her about the feelings she's likely to have mentally which is normal. If she's not comfortable talking to me, she needs to talk to Tyler or Sophie or Roxanne or Megan or you, so she gets the help she needs. Then, I have to call Tyler before Dany does. Then, you and I need to talk about you putting yourself in danger and not letting me know. Ette, it could have gone bad, really bad. You can't do that again."

"I couldn't let your chance with Dany go. It's my fault John came here in the first place."

"We had it covered."

"I also couldn't let Sophie get herself into something that could have taken her away from Gaige. Have you seen the way he looks at her? It's the stuff dreams are made of."

He inhaled but didn't say anything. He noticed it. The way Gaige looked at Sophie and the way she looked at him. It was the stuff dreams were made of. To have someone's love shine on you was special. To have it shine on you so noticeably that everyone could see it, well that was something.

"We'll chat about it later. After Dany falls asleep, come to my room."

He kissed the top of her head and was relieved she didn't argue. Stepping into the elevator he looked Dany in the eye. "Let's go to the clinic so I can make sure everything is good."

"Okay." Dany was quiet, he locked eyes with her to make sure she wasn't going to pass out or anything, but he didn't want to embarrass her. So, he turned to the door as it closed and waited the few seconds until the door opened again on the conference room floor.

Taking Yvette's hand, he pulled her along. He stopped just outside of the elevator to wait for Dany, then moved forward when she began making her way to the clinic.

Opening the door, the lights clicked on and he immediately walked to the counter and pulled the stethoscope from the top drawer.

"Take a seat on the table, Dany," he said without looking. He pulled some Ibuprofen out and dropped two tablets into a paper cup, then turned to see Yvette standing next to Dany holding her hands.

Dang, that made his heart skip a beat. Yvette looked tired and so did Dany. They'd both been through more than most humans will go through in their lifetimes.

He wet some tissues and handed them to Yvette, motioning around his face. She took them, and walked to the wall across from the sink, and looked into the mirror.

Quickly she began wiping the blood spatter from her face.

He listened to Dany's heartbeat, took her pulse, and looked into her eyes. Her pupils were still slow to respond, but that was normal. They'd come back after some rest.

"Tell me how you feel."

Dany shrugged. "Dry mouth like I've eaten a bail of cotton. Slight headache. My arm is sore."

She pointed to her upper left arm and he could see redness where they'd undoubtedly not been all that careful with the needle.

He handed her the paper cup with the Ibuprofen, walked to the mini fridge, and pulled out a bottle of water, untwisted the cap, and handed it to her.

"Go up to your room, take a shower, then get some rest. Some things to be aware of Dany, since we don't know what drugs they gave you. You may have diarrhea, stomach cramps, anxiety, vomiting and irritability. That's if they used opioid based drugs. Let me know if any of those things happen and I'll likely have something to help relieve the symptoms. They are temporary so that's a bonus."

"Shit, Dad, you make it all sound so sexy."

She called him dad again and he'd be lying if he said that didn't affect him. Hearing that made his heart swell tenfold. He leaned in and wrapped his arms around her. Her arms quickly came around his waist and he enjoyed holding his daughter. It did something to him. It made him feel almost whole. Or complete, was that it? Something had been missing in him and now it felt almost filled. He didn't have the beautiful words to explain it.

"Okay." He kissed her temple. "Go on up and get yourself tucked into bed. Call me if you need anything. Or you can let Yvette know, too. But I want to know if you need anything. Got it?"

"Got it." She genuinely smiled at him and his heart swelled again. Is that what happened when father's daughters smiled at them? The term "wrapped around her little finger" came to mind and now he understood it.

She scooted off the table and looked at Yvette.

"Are you coming up right away?"

He spoke for Yvette. "No, I need to check her knees out and make sure they're okay, then she needs to come to the debriefing. We have to talk about what will happen next because of Caulfield's death."

"He died?"

Yvette nodded her head, the expression on her face sad.

"I kill..." She swallowed. "Because of me."

"You killed him?" Dany's expression showed her disbelief.

"I had to help get you back."

"You really helped to save me?"

Dany leaned forward and grabbed Yvette with both arms. They hugged for a long time and he couldn't look away. This right here felt like his family. These two got along great. The way he felt just watching them, even though it surprised the shit out of him, made him feel...fantastic. These two women... ah, it was perfect.

He heard Dany whisper, "Thank you, Ette. Thank you so much."

Yvette's eyes closed, the tears rolled down her cheeks as she held his daughter, and he knew her feelings were pure.

His phone vibrated and he looked down to see a text. "Team meeting in five."

[illegible] them. She [illegible] and waved her [illegible] over at them she smiled and [illegible] then stepped into the elevator.

"She's a sweet girl." She told Wyatt.

"She is."

He stopped them at the conference room door and turned her to face him.

"Wh[illegible] I'm her [illegible] for now. With you. Do you understand?"

She swallowed the lump in her throat.

"Yes."

He leaned down and brushed his lips to hers, then opened the conference room door and stepped back so she could enter ahead of him.

Most of the team was already in place. Jax rushed up to her and hugged her tightly. Enjoying the feeling of her friend's hug was a balm in and of itself. Hugging her back she tried pulling strength from Jax. This woman was her role model.

Jax pulled back and looked at her. "How are you?"

She chuckled. "I'm fine. Tired. Sore. Maybe a bit numb."

"Understandable."

"How are you? You've been so tired lately. Are you feeling better?"

"I am. We'll chat about that in a minute. First, let's debrief."

Jax let her go and turned to Wyatt. She held out her right hand to shake his.

"I'm so sorry, Wyatt. I fucked up and I'll struggle to forgive myself forever."

Wyatt hesitated only a moment, then reached out and pulled Jax in for a hug. It made her feel good that there weren't any hard feelings. She knew he had been pissed at her.

"It's all good, Jax. You're one of the best operatives I know and have had the pleasure of working with. I don't blame you."

"You did."

"I did but now I know better."

Jax pulled back and socked him in the arm and everyone in the room laughed and Gaige started in

"Okay, so here's what I have so far. On our way back I called Casper who called the local authorities. Locals got there just as the buyer was rolling in and a shootout took place. They got one, two escaped. They are willing, with some convincing and cajoling from Casper, to let this look as if Caulfield and his buyer had a serious disagreement and shot it out. This isn't something we can count on happening every time, but Casper is aware of what we were up against and whatever deals he's making with the locals, that's between them. He made some reference to favors being owed and called. None of our business."

Gaige looked at her, "No charges will be brought against you, Yvette."

Biting her lips together she nodded but words wouldn't come out. Taking a few deep breaths, she mouthed, "Thank you."

Wyatt's arm wrapped her into a hug and pulled her close to his body. She buried her face into his chest and let him support her weight while she gathered herself together.

Gaige continued, "Now, that said, Yvette, never do that again. We had a plan and you interrupted it causing us to have to change mid-stream. That put Sophie and Dany's lives in danger."

"I'm so sorry." She finally managed and Wyatt squeezed her shoulders.

Sophie winked at her from across the room and Jax nodded. Apparently owning up and being sorry was what they needed. Gaige continued telling them what worked and what didn't and how they may play something like this in the future. She quietly listened her mind all over the board on what she was hearing, and their tactics being discussed. But a couple of things struck her. Gaige listened to everyone when they had something to say. The whole team was supportive of each other and offered constructive criticism if it was needed. Aside from the general ball-breaking they were respectful of each other which showed her just how these men and women made this work.

Gaige ended their meeting. "Okay, let's get some sleep. My future wife and I have guests coming and a wedding to finish prepping for."

"Wait." Dodge halted everyone. "Jax and I have something to say."

He looked down at her and when she looked up at him, there it was, that look. They loved each other. They were also stunning together. He so blond and fair and she with her olive complexion and shiny black hair, they were the perfect complement to the other.

Jax turned. "I've been tired and dragging ass lately and I finally went to the doctor this morning." She looked up at Dodge again. Her smile breathtaking. His genuine and pure.

Dodge kissed her lips briefly then turned to the group. "We're going to be parents."

Yvette gasped and ran around the table to hug her friend. All around them congratulations were being exchanged with Dodge, but Jax held her close and whispered in her ear. "I hope you'll be his Godmother."

Yvette cried into her friend's shoulder. "Yes, of course." She squeezed Jax then pulled back without letting go. "How do you know already it's a boy?"

"A girl would not make me so fucking exhausted all the time. Men, they can be exhausting."

They both laughed and Sophie came over to hug Jax. It gave Yvette time to swipe at her tears and under her eyes so hopefully she didn't have dark smudges of mascara streaking.

Wyatt stepped up behind her and hugged Jax once again while telling her what a badass mom she was going to be.

Josh stepped forward and hugged his sister and brother-in-law while asking, "How did Mama take the news that she was going to be an abuela?"

Jax's eyes rounded. "I haven't told her yet."

"Jacqueline Masters Sager. She is going to kick your ass."

Jax just shrugged and smiled at her brother. "Uncle Josh can help protect me."

"Oh my gosh, I'm going to be a tío."

He scooped Jax up in his arms and swung her around. "Tío!" His laugh was genuine. "I'm going to be Uncle Josh."

...ing. Yvette's ... over where she ...

"I'd just to check on her," he said softly. "But I'd love it if you came back to my room with me tonight."

She looked up at him, a soft smile on her face, her tawny eyes locked on his. "Okay," she whispered back.

Waving her card in front of the door she opened it quietly and he followed her in ...

Dany lay sleeping, curled up into a ball, under the covers. The aroma of soap and slight humidity in the air told him she'd done as he asked, showered and tucked in.

Leaning over he lay his hand on her forehead and was relieved there was no fever. Staring at her in slumber for a few moment's he thought how proud Susanna would be to see their daughter all grown up and beautiful.

He turned to see Yvette smiling as she watched him. He nodded and they left the room as quietly as they'd come in. He took her hand and led her across the hall and down to the next door. Waving his card to allow them entry, he pushed the door open and allowed Yvette to step inside ahead of him. She stopped just inside the door and looked around the room. Standing behind her he wrapped his arms around her and waited for her to take it all in.

Turning in his arms she kissed his lips softly. "Do you mind if I shower?"

"Of course not." He pointed to the bathroom and she disappeared behind the door.

Sitting on his sofa, he pulled off his boots and sat back resting his head and closing his eyes. The soft sounds of the shower running, and thoughts of Yvette's wet body invaded his mind and caused his body to stir. He liked that feeling. The anticipation of being with a woman he genuinely had feelings for. And he did. Somehow in the matter of a few days she'd wiggled under his skin and took hold.

The shower shut off and he leaned forward scraping his hands through his hair. Standing, he pulled his t-shirt over his head and tossed it in the clothes hamper alongside the bathroom door. Unbuckling his belt and unzipping his pants, he stopped short when Yvette stepped from the bathroom smelling like heaven and looking like sin. She was wrapped in a towel, but her long brunette hair flowed down her back and over her shoulders. Her skin was still damp from the shower and she smelled delicious.

Stepping to him, she raised up on her toes and kissed his lips softly, then went past him and walked to the bed. Suddenly he wasn't feeling so tired.

Quickly ducking into the shower and turning the

water on, he divested himself of the rest of his clothing and stepped under the warm water. Thoughts of Yvette laying in his bed had certain parts of his body standing at attention and his mind had a difficult time thinking about anything else.

Rinsing off he stepped out of the shower, grabbed a towel from the rack, and hand dried his hair and body. Wrapping the towel around his waist he stepped into the bedroom and his eyes landed on Yvette, sitting up with her back against the headboard, texting on her phone. Her eyes looked into his and she smiled.

"Just telling Jax once more how excited I am for her."

Reaching over she lay her phone on the bedside table and looked up at him. Flipping the light switch off, he dropped his towel and slid into bed alongside Yvette and his heart felt whole. Turning into his arms, their naked bodies touching he kissed her soft lips as his hands floated over as much of her body as he could touch. Stopping at her ass to pull her in tight, the feel of her curls touching the tip of his cock caused him to twitch and Yvette pushed into him harder.

Rolling her to her back, he kissed along her jaw, her neck, across her chest until he found a perfectly pointed nipple and sucked it into his mouth. His hand continued to roam down her torso, hip and across to those luscious curls between her legs and a thrill ran through him as she spread herself open for him. His fingers entered her, and she softly moaned, and he didn't know what was better, the soft sounds she made, the sound of her wetness or the way she felt circling around his fingers. Ultimately, that won out because his cock wanted to feel that. Promising to take his time with her tomorrow, he rose slightly, positioned his cock at her entrance and looked into her eyes. The soft light from the moon shining in gave her an ethereal glow, but her eyes, those light tawny eyes were trained on his.

She softly said, "We weren't responsible before, but I'm on birth control and I'm clean."

"I know. I let my emotions get the better of me and I apologize for that. I'm clean as well but will use a condom if you prefer."

Her head shook slowly. She whispered, "No."

Slowly entering her while staring into her eyes, he watched as her lips turned into a soft smile as the feeling of their bodies joining together washed over both of them.

Her body accepted his as he slid out and back in until he was fully inside of her. Her legs instinctively raised up and wrapped around his ass and he pushed into her again and again, their bodies each pleasing the other. The soft sounds she made each time he pushed into her made his heart beat faster and his new favorite sound was Yvette's erotic whimpers as her hips rose to accept him inside.

Their dance pace accelerated as their bodies sought relief. His balls began to draw up painfully into his body and the drive to seek release urged him on. He ground his hips against her clit each time he pushed all the way into her, and her sounds changed as they increased in intensity.

"Yes." She whispered and he knew she was close. Hopefully, she'd get there before him because he was so fucking close.

Her lips formed the perfect 'O' as she gasped out a moan, her body stiffened with her release and he felt elated as he allowed himself his own release. The fire spewing from the tip of his cock, the tightness in his balls, an instant of pain followed by relief. He twitched as he came, his arms shook as he held himself over her body, his mind, well it was rather blank at the moment.

weight ... reached up to ... and her hand found firm ... close to her ear helped her mind begin to clear. She'd spent the night with Wyatt. Actually, after they made love last night, he'd scooped her into his arms and pulled her back to his body, and she didn't remember anything after that. She remembered feeling loved and happy and ...

Voices from below floated up to her, though not clearly, and she couldn't make out words. She listened for a time, then a gruff sleep sated voice in her ear said, "Gaige's sister and her family must be here."

The wedding. Tomorrow was the wedding and this place would be buzzing today.

"Have you ever met them?"

"Yep." He kissed her cheek then rolled to his back. They were here a few months ago, for Dodge and Jax's wedding. Their kids weren't with them though. I haven't seen them in a number of years."

He sat up and she admired his back. Strong muscles bunched and stretched as he moved.

"Dane was one of the founders of GHOST. It was because of Keirnan, did you know that?"

She searched her mind as she rolled to her side to face him. "No, I didn't know that. What happened?"

"She was kidnapped by an enemy of her father's. She and Dane had just started dating. Dane and Auggie, Keirnan and Gaige's father, worked together to rescue her. Shortly afterward Keirnan and Dane were married, and Dane and Auggie started GHOST."

"Wow." She stared into the amber eyes that stared back at her and she thought he was the most beautiful man she'd ever known.

He leaned over, his weight on his elbow and looked deeply into her eyes. "You keep looking at me like that, Ette, and I'll be making you mine again."

"Please tell me what that look is like because then I'll keep doing it. But just so we're clear, I believe I'm making you mine."

He leaned down and kissed her lips. Not all soft and slow this time but fast, harder than before and more urgency in his kiss as he shoved his hands under her and pulled her close before rolling over with Yvette on top.

Pushing up so she was looking down at him his grin said volumes as to his playfulness at the moment.

"You want to make me yours, baby, I'd say climb on and show me how it's done."

Pulling her hair back so her breasts were exposed to him she licked her lips and fondled them while he watched. Pinching her nipples until they were firm and pronounced, she felt his cock thicken and lengthen under her and she smiled.

Interested in his body, she scooted down so his cock was in full view and she looked at him. All of him, then wrapped her hands around it and pumped it a few times. The shiny silver balls on his penis caught her attention and she rolled her thumb over them.

"Is this piercing for you or the women you're with?"

He hesitated before answering. "It's for me. It tugs a bit when I'm inside which is an interesting sensation. Does it do anything for you?"

"I guess I can feel it a little but not that it makes a big difference. What made you decide to do this?"

"I was drunk one night, and a friend dared me."

She chuckled and rolled her thumb over the shiny orbs again and his cock twitched in her hand.

"Did it hurt?"

"Not at the time I was pretty hammered."

She slowly rose up and placed the head of his cock at her opening. Staring into his eyes she slid slowly down on him enjoying the pleasure she saw on his face. His black hair and beard against the contrast of his light amber eyes were stunning. The smile on his face as she sank down on him was one she wanted to see over and over again.

Once she was all the way down on him, she ground herself against him, back and forth a few times, taking ultimate pleasure in the feel of him inside of her. His strong hands rested on her hips and he added a bit of pressure and his hips rose up, so he was fully inside of her.

She began riding him, enjoying all of him, the way he looked, the smile on his face, the look in his eyes, the shape of his body, the tattoos on his arms and hands, the smattering of hair across his chest and his muscles as they bunched as he exerted himself. Placing her right hand over his heart, she enjoyed feeling the beat as it increased as their lovemaking became more passionate, their pace quickened.

Her climax was beginning to wash over her, her skin heated and dampened as the heat in the room grew warmer. Placing both hands on his chest she enjoyed the pleasure she got from his body and frankly she enjoyed him. The man who was Wyatt.

Her breathing was choppy when she asked, "Are you close?"

His grip on her hips tightened as he ground out, "Fuck yes."

She rode him like the finish line couldn't come soon enough. Their pace increased and they each exerted maximum effort in pleasuring the other. Her heartbeat became different just now. While it beat faster, its beat was now full. Her heart was full. This moment made an indelible mark in her life because she realized right this moment that she loved this man. Their sex wasn't just that. Not for her anyway. She wanted him to receive pleasure from her in a way that no one else had ever given him pleasure.

She wanted them to come together, but she couldn't hold out. Her orgasm washed over her like a wildfire over dried sticks. The flames licked her, and she cried out his name as she came. And her body held stock still for a fraction of a second before he'd tossed her over and wildly raced to his completion, groaning her name in her ear as he spilled into her.

the hall to the room she
with Dany. She emerged a few minutes later
dressed in a cute little spring dress and sandals.

"Dany must be downstairs," she said as she grabbed his hand. Somehow, she looked more gorgeous than she had prior to today. Most of her bruising was fading, her knees in the parking lot last night. It was the smile on her face and the happiness she exuded that changed her appearance.

She looked up at him, "How are you this morning?"

He chuckled. "I'm fine."

As they neared the bottom of the stairs the voices grew louder and laughter filled the air. Turning the corner to head back to the dining room he squeezed Yvette's hand before they walked in. She looked up at him and smiled and he felt like a young man falling in love for the first time.

"There they are. Dad, come in and see Dane and Keirnan."

Dane approached him with a smile on his face and his hand held out to shake. As soon as their hands touched, Dane pulled him in for a hug.

"Heard you had quite the night last night."

His face flamed red. He knew Dane was talking about the mission, but his thoughts went to making love with Yvette. That's what it felt like now. More than sex. The little vixen had made him hers.

"We did." He looked at Yvette. "Dane, this is Yvette."

Dane shook her hand. "It's nice to meet you, Yvette. Dany and Jax have been filling us in on you and your mission last night."

Yvette chuckled. "Not sure I was on an actual mission, at least not a GHOST mission. But I went willingly and with purpose, but I think that was my last mission. I don't have the wherewithal for it."

Keirnan hugged him tightly. "It's nice to see you again, Wyatt."

As gorgeous as ever, her blond hair and dark green eyes were lively and happy. "Can you believe my big brother is finally going to marry Sophie? I had given up all hope."

Keirnan's beautiful smile landed on Yvette. "It's a pleasure to meet the woman who finally captured Wyatt's heart, Yvette. I look forward to getting to know you better. You must be something special indeed."

Yvette's face turned a bright red, her mouth opened then closed then opened again. "It's so nice to meet you, Keirnan. I'm not sure you're right about me, but I do look forward to getting to know you as well."

Then a beautiful young woman with long dark curly hair, deep brown eyes and the most perfect smile walked up to them and looked at him waiting for him to recognize her. He did of course. He'd recognize her anywhere; she was the spitting image of her father and she was strikingly beautiful.

"Emmy, you've grown up. Do I hug you or salute you now?"

She laughed. "A hug would be great. I don't outrank you. Yet."

He laughed and wrapped her in a hug. "I'm sure you will one day."

"Emmy, this is Yvette."

Emmy turned and hugged Yvette. "It's nice to meet you. I've heard all about you from Dany."

Yvette's face continued to stay red. "I'm afraid to ask, so I won't. It's nice to meet you as well. Where are you stationed?"

"Fort Jackson. I'm deploying to Afghanistan in October though."

Dane and Keirnan's other two children, well, young adults, Hayden and Elise came to meet them. Hayden was 20 now and Elise now 19 were both in the service. Both carried the family genes beautifully, Hayden also looked like Emmy with the dark hair and eyes. Elise was a Vickers through and through with her blond hair and green sparkling eyes. It caused him to look across the room at Dany chatting with Sophie and Jax. He saw Susanna in her. Her smile and the shape of her eyes, but her coloring was him. Dark hair and light amber eyes. Pride swelled through him. She was a lovely young woman, though he couldn't take credit for anything more than her genes. Tyler had raised her, and he made a mental note to call her and thank her once again for the fantastic job she had done.

Wedding talk was the topic of the day but as soon as breakfast was over, Gaige pulled him aside.

"I don't want to talk shop now, but as soon as I get back from my honeymoon, we do need to talk. There is a buyer out there who feels cheated. Casper has been watching him on the internet and he's been squawking about being cheated. Apparently, he'd already sent Caulfield money for Dany and Sophie after seeing their pictures. While I'm gone, you need to keep a close eye on Dany."

His eyes naturally drifted across the room where Dany and Yvette chatted with Keirnan and Emmy.

"I will. What about Yvette?"

"No word on her. Doesn't mean she isn't a target though."

"Thanks. I'll be careful and we'll stick close to home base. When you get back, we'll have a plan and run it by you for tweaking or approval as to how to end this. My first thought is why can't the authorities force Caulfield's estate to reimburse him?"

"I asked that question and I guess in this nasty underworld of human trafficking, it's the principal of the thing. If this guy gets stiffed, someone else will try it and then someone else, so he has to make an example out of this situation. Even though Caulfield is dead, there is always a number two thinking he'll step in. Plus, I doubt the executor can legally pay someone for illegal conduct."

"Jesus."

"Yeah."

"Gaige, we need to get the arbor in place and decorated." Sophie came over to them and smiled lovingly at Gaige and he visibly melted.

Gaige whistled loudly, "All hands on deck everyone we've got some wedding decorating to do."

Yvette walked to him and placed her hand on his chest. "Is everything alright? You look worried."

"I'm fine, Yvette but you, Dany, and I need to have a chat later."

45

Wyatt and ... to a chair. It ... over it was impossible ... forever and there wasn't a plan yet. She could tell Wyatt didn't want to tell them this. His mood had been dark all afternoon. She'd been worried about what had happened but didn't want to nag him. Now that rehearsal was over and almost everyone was either visiting and lounging in the living room or had gone to bed, they had the time to discuss their situation.

"Does this mean I can't go home on Monday?"

"Yes, it does Dany. I'm sorry, I know you have a flight scheduled, but until we know you'll be safe, we can't risk it. When are you supposed to start college?"

Dany scooted forward in her chair. "Dad, I'm not going to college. Not directly anyway." She paused and Wyatt's brows rose high.

"I thought you..."

"I do but hear me out. I want to join the Army. I want to go to nursing school in the service and maybe become a doctor. I've been chatting with Emmy, Hayden and Elise a lot today and I want to be like them. I want to serve. And, by doing that, I'll be better able to protect myself from assholes like these shitty traffickers."

Wyatt leaned forward and placed his elbows on his knees.

"Dany, are you sure you understand the commitment that will require?"

"I am. Dad, I've never been so excited in my life. I feel this in my bones. I feel it with everything I have. I want to follow in your and my mother's footsteps. It makes me feel whole just thinking about it."

Wyatt turned his head and looked at Yvette but said nothing. Dany leaned over closer to Yvette then and took her hand.

"Ette, tell him it's a good idea."

"Oh no you don't. Don't drag me into this. I'm no one who should have an opinion. I'm not family or anything and you need to make this decision for yourself."

Dany looked at her in disbelief. "You're kidding, right? Have you seen the way he looks at you? Have you seen the way you look at him? You two have that thing. That look. That something something."

Pulling her phone up Dany tapped a couple of icons and scrolled through her pictures. She turned her phone to her and Wyatt, and Yvette's jaw fell open. There they were, Wyatt and she, talking to Axel, Dodge and Jax and laughing, but she and Wyatt were looking at each other. Each of them looking at the other as if they were the only person in the world.

Dany swiped and another picture showed up from this afternoon outside as they placed the tables and chairs around the yard. Wyatt was talking to Sophie, getting directions and Yvette was looking at him. She had that look. It was there and she didn't even know it. Did people know when they had it?

"So, now tell me what you think. Please."

She bit her bottom lip as she gathered her thoughts.

"Dany. I think the service is an honorable thing to do. But only if you're sure you can commit to it fully and embrace it. It's not an easy life and Emmy said she's being deployed this fall. What if you're deployed? You won't be able to come home. How will your mom feel about this?"

Dany looked between her father and her. "Look. What if I promise to think about this for the week? I'll do some research and I'll check out all the MOS's and see what's offered to me and when. Then, let's talk about this in a week and if I still feel strongly about it, will you give me your blessing?"

Looking at Wyatt, he nodded, "If you give it thought, and do your due diligence, I will gladly give you my blessing. But you should get Tyler's blessing, too. She's raised you. I'll speak to her on your behalf if you need me to."

Dany's smile broadened and she clapped her hands together. Turning to her, she continued, "Yvette?"

"Yes. If you are still as excited about this after all of your research, I will give you my blessing. Even though you don't need it."

Dany jumped up and hugged Wyatt. She leaned over and kissed Yvette's cheek and turned to leave the room. Before making it to the door, she stopped and said, "I also promise not to leave the compound this week while you all come up with a plan, I'll do my research.

She turned and left the room and she and Wyatt sat in silence for a few minutes. He leaned down and kissed her softly, then he chuckled as their lips were touching.

"I think you love me."

His lips molded to hers once again and she whispered against his lips, "I think you love me."

His arm snaked out and wrapped around her waist, pulling her closer. He pulled his lips away from hers and looked into her eyes for a long time. No hardship there, she could look into his eyes forever. Those eyes were framed with dark thick lashes. And the tiny lines at the corners of his eyes added maturity and life.

"I do love you, Yvette. You snuck up on me though, I wasn't looking to fall in love, I thought I had everything I needed here. I didn't realize I was missing anything until you and Dany came into my life. And now, well, here we are. I love you."

"Wow. That's...amazing." She cleared her throat "I love you, too, Wyatt. And clearly I didn't come here looking for love. But there you were standing in the airport, helping a bedraggled, terrified woman you didn't know to help a friend. What an amazing man you are."

46

love and happiness in this room for two people was what everyone dreamed of. They'd had a journey, these two, but they seemed to finally be on the way to their happily ever after. Six months ago, Wyatt would have scoffed at the idea of that. Six days ago, he'd have said happiness like this in life was bliss reserved for only a select few people in this world.

He felt twitchy. He'd not slept well last night. The only thing that helped him was when he awoke in the middle of the night and Yvette would sweetly roll over and wrap her arms around him. His heart settled and sleep found him, but not for long.

Now standing outside of the compound looking over the grounds Sophie had so painstakingly made them help her with, he tried to puzzle out why he felt unsettled today. There was a madman still out there, but madmen were always out there; it's how he made his living.

"What's got you all down in the mouth?" Axel came to stand next to him, both of them now surveying the grounds from their vantage point.

"I don't know. That's what I was trying to figure out. I didn't sleep last night. I think it's too much change. Gaige and Sophie, even though they've been here together for close to a year, they are now married. Dodge and Jax are having babies. Dany and I have become friends and she's now calling me dad. And Yvette. Her life is still a bit unsettled but now mine feels unsettled, too."

"Nothing stays the same for long. As we all get older, we have to deal with change more than ever. Look at us all, Wyatt. We're all in our late thirties and forties. Time marches on. In our line of work, we lose people we love, we mourn, we marry - though not me for fucks sake, but those guys." He nodded toward their comrades who stood about drinking and enjoying themselves. "And life goes by in the blink of an eye."

"Yeah." He took a drink of the beer in his hand and watched Dany laughing with Megan and Skye. "I guess for so long I thought this is the way it would be for me. But it's all the changes and they're all out of my control."

"Yep. Back in the day I thought I'd get married and have kids and get a grunt job like my old man, but life had other plans for me. Now I get to shoot guns, play with cool gadgets, and help people who need help." Axel's voice grew pensive.

"Right."

Dodge leaned over and kissed the top of Jax's head, then lay his hand over her belly; though it was still flat, it would soon be burgeoning with child.

Axel slapped him on the back, "Come on sad sack, let's

go enjoy our friends and celebrate our boss getting a boss." He laughed and Wyatt couldn't help but laugh with him.

"Yeah, I'll be right there, I have something to do first."

Axel walked across the lawn and started chatting with Josh and Ford and he scanned the lawn for Yvette. Seeing her chatting with Keirnan and Emmy, he walked in their direction. Yvette looked up and saw him approach and the smile that she bestowed on him was like she'd just lit his path, a beacon guiding him home. That's when it hit him.

Kissing her lips, he whispered, "Do you have a minute to chat?"

"Of course."

He nodded to Keirnan and Emmy, "I hope you ladies don't mind if I steal Yvette for a moment."

Keirnan laughed. "Of course not, we have plenty of people we haven't seen in some time. We'll chat later."

Pulling Yvette close to his body he steered her to a private corner of the yard, close to the trees Jax, Josh, Dodge, and Sophie had planted. The bench in front of them sat empty and he motioned for her to sit down.

"I've been trying to puzzle out why I was so restless last night and today and it just hit me. I think I feel unsettled because you're unsettled."

Her brows bunched but he quickly kissed the crease between them and moved back to look into her eyes.

"We don't always know what life has in store for us and, honestly, a week ago I thought my life was the way it was going to be until my knee gave me enough grief that I'd have to retire. I've saved up over the years and clearly, I don't have living expenses here so saving was rather easy. Plus, we had a very big job recently and the cut each of us received was unbelievable. Ask Jax about her rings from Dodge."

"Wyatt, you're making me nervous. Are you asking me to leave?"

"No, I'm asking you to stay. I'm making a mess of it, I'm afraid. But Yvette..." He swallowed the lump in his throat. Until this very moment it never occurred to him that she could say no. Scraping his hand through his hair, he twisted on the bench, so he was facing her head on.

"Yvette, I don't know how long we'd stay here, in this house surrounded by these people. It might be a year, two years, maybe only two months for all we know. But then I'll have to move on from here and live out my days, hopefully playing with grandchildren that Dany makes for me and enjoying my days. But with all of those uncertainties the one thing I know with absolutely certainty is I want you with me. Whether it be here or in a house on a lake with a dog or two."

She swallowed but her eyes never looked away from his. "I want to be with you, too, Wyatt. I don't care where we're at either. I feel like I'm home with you, the location is just a detail."

He laughed. "Let's make it official then." He knelt in front of her. "Yvette Jacobsen, will you marry me? Will you face the future with me as my wife?"

"Wyatt Lawson, I absolutely will marry you."

He pulled her close and kissed her lips. Then she giggled.

"I can't believe it. I'm going to be a wife and a Godmother soon."

He chuckled, "I can't believe I'm going to be a husband and my daughter is here with us."

They laughed, then he stood and took her hand.

"We'll go shopping for a ring to make it official, but right now let's go tell Dany, then the others."

Axel is about to meet the two most important people in his life - even though he doesn't know one of them exists. Read Defending Bridget by clicking this link - - > https://books2read.com/u/3yKjoZ

ENJOY THIS BOOK? YOU CAN MAKE A BIG DIFFERENCE

Reviews are the most powerful tools in my arsenal when it comes to getting attention for my books. As much as I'd like to, I don't have the financial muscle of a New York publisher. I can't take out full page ads in the newspaper or put posters on the subway.

(Not yet, anyway.)

But I do have something much more powerful and effective than that, and it's something that those big publishers would die to get their hands on.

A committed and loyal bunch of readers.

Honest reviews of my books help bring them to the attention of other readers.

If you've enjoyed this book I would be so grateful to you if you could spend just five minutes leaving a review (it can be as short as you like) on the book's vendor page. You can jump right to the page of your choice by clicking below.

<u>Thank you so very much.</u>

ALSO BY PJ FIALA

You can find all of my books at https://pjfiala.com/books

Romantic Suspense

Rolling Thunder Series

Moving to Love, Book 1

Moving to Hope, Book 2

Moving to Forever, Book 3

Moving to Desire, Book 4

Moving to You, Book 5

Moving On, Book 6

Rolling Thunder Boxset 1, Books 1-3

Rolling Thunder Boxset 2, Books 4-6

Military Romantic Suspense

Second Chances Series

Designing Samantha's Love, Book 1

Securing Kiera's Love, Book 2

Bluegrass Security Series

Heart Thief, Book One

Finish Line, Book Two

Lethal Love, Book Three

Wrenched Fate, Book Four

Lynyrd Station Protectors - Security

Finding His Fire Book One

Finding His Mark Book Two

Finding His Jewel Book Three

Finding His Match Book Four

Lynyrd Station Protectors - Special Ops

Defending Keirnan, GHOST Book One

Defending Sophie, GHOST Book Two

Defending Roxanne, GHOST Book Three

Defending Yvette, GHOST Book Four

Defending Bridget, GHOST Book Five

Defending Isabella, GHOST Book Six

GHOST Box Set One (Books 1-3)

GHOST Box Set Two (Books 4-6)

Lynyrd Station Protectors - Trafficking

RAPTOR Rising - Prequel

Saving Shelby, RAPTOR Book One

Holding Hadleigh, RAPTOR Book Two

Craving Charlesia, RAPTOR Book Three

Promising Piper, RAPTOR Book Four

Missing Mia, RAPTOR Book Five

Believing Becca, RAPTOR Book Six

Keeping Kori, RAPTOR Book Seven

Healing Hope, RAPTOR Book Eight

Engaging Emersyn, RAPTOR Book Nine

RAPTOR Box Set 1

RAPTOR Box Set 2

RAPTOR Box Set 3

GHOST Legacy (Next generation)

Finding Lara, Book One

Saving Elena, Book Two

Rescuing Kenna, Book Three

Protecting Everleigh, Book Four

Guarding Adelaide, Book Five

Shielding Maya, Book Six

MEET PJ

Writing has been a desire my whole life. Once I found the courage to write, life changed for me in the most profound way. Bringing stories to readers that I'd enjoy reading and creating characters that are flawed, but lovable is such a joy.

When not writing, I'm with my family doing something fun. My husband, Gene, and I are bikers and enjoy riding to new locations, meeting new people and generally enjoying this fabulous country we live in.

I come from a family of veterans. My grandfather, father, brother, two sons, and one daughter-in-law are all veterans. Needless to say, I am proud to be an American and proud of the service my amazing family has given.

PJ is the author of the exciting Rolling Thunder series, Big 3 Security series, Second Chances series, Bluegrass Security series and GHOST series which enthrall readers with page turning military alphas and the women who love them.

Her online home is https://www.pjfiala.com.
You can connect with PM on Facebook at https://www.
facebook.com/PJFiala,

on Twitter at @pfiala and
Instagram at https://www.Instagram.com/PJFiala.
If you prefer to email, go ahead, she'll respond - pjfiala@
pjfiala.com.

COPYRIGHT

Printed in the United States of America

First published 2020

Fiala, PJ

DEFENDING YVETTE / PJ Fiala

p. cm.

1. Romance—Fiction. 2. Romance—Suspense. 3. Romance - Military

I. Title – DEFENDING YVETTE

ISBN-13: 978-1-942618-53-9